THIS CHILD MUST DIE

CLEOPAS LUMBANTOBING, CHALLENGER OF DEMONS, EVANGELIST,
EDUCATOR AND PEACEMAKER TO THE WARRING BATAKS OF NORTH SUMATRA

A BIOGRAPHY BY

ANNE RUCK

Based on an Indonesian original

AN OMF BOOK

English edition published by
Overseas Missionary Fellowship (IHQ) Ltd
(*formerly China Inland Mission*)
2 Cluny Road, Singapore 1025, Republic of Singapore

First English edition 1991

OMF books are distributed by
OMF, 10 West Dry Creek Circle, Littleton, CO 80120-4427, USA
OMF, Belmont, The Vine, Sevenoaks, Kent TN13 3TZ, UK
OMF, P O Box 849, Epping, NSW 2121, Australia
OMF, 1058 Avenue Road, Toronto, Ontario M5N 2C6, Canada
OMF, P O Box 10159, Auckland, New Zealand
OMF, P O Box 41, Kenilworth 7745, South Africa
and other OMF offices

Cover design by Steve Eames

ISBN 981-3009-01-2

CONTENTS

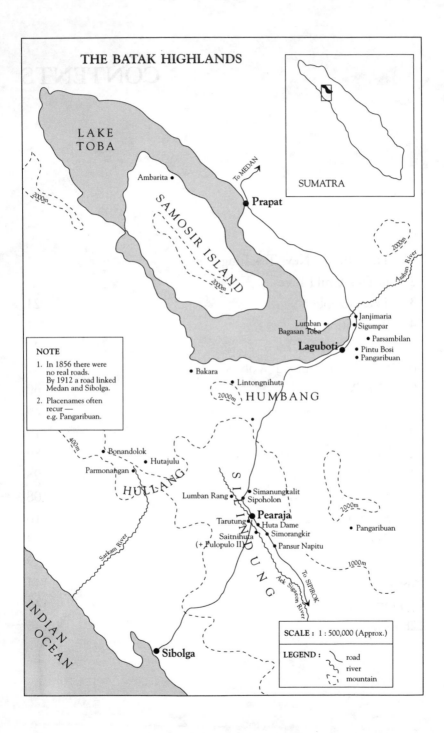

THE BATAK HIGHLANDS

SUMATRA

LAKE TOBA

Ambarita •

To MEDAN

■ **Prapat**

SAMOSIR ISLAND

2000m

2000m

2000m

Asahan River

2000m

Lumban •
Bagasan Toba

Janjimaria •
Sigumpar •

• Parsambilan

Laguboti■

• Pintu Bosi
• Pangaribuan

NOTE

1. In 1856 there were
   no real roads.
   By 1912 a road linked
   Medan and Sibolga.

2. Placenames often
   recur —
   e.g. Pangaribuan.

• Bakara

• Lintongnihuta

2000m **HUMBANG**

400m

• Bonandolok

• Hutajulu

Parmonangan •

H U L L A N G

2000m

S I

Lumban Rang •

• Simanungkalit
Sipoholon

U

Pearaja■

Tarutung • • Huta Dame
• Simorangkir

Saitnihuta
(+ Pulopulo II) • Pansur Napitu

• Pangaribuan

N

Sarkam River

1000m

G

Aek Sigeon River

To SIPIROK

INDIAN OCEAN

■ **Sibolga**

SCALE : 1 : 500,000 (Approx.)

LEGEND : road
river
mountain

PROLOGUE
SILINDUNG 1856

The datu[1] sat cross-legged, gazing in horror at the elaborate diagram traced out on the ground in front of him. In his hand he held a bamboo cylinder, and once more he ran his fingers down the markings of the Batak calendar: here the scorpion's pincers, there his tail, there the day that kicks and butts like an angry water-buffalo. Turning to the bark-leaved augury book at his side he found the drawing of the compass-points. For the fifth time he repeated his calculations. There could be no mistake.

Ompu Ginjang, the raja, watched him closely. It was the raja's newborn son whose fate was being predicted, and Ginjang longed for a promise that his lands and his power would be extended through this child. He had two sons already, and so far the spirits had promised nothing. But for this, his third son?

The datu sat musing in silence. Clearly he was afraid to tell what he saw.

"What is it?" snapped Ginjang impatiently. "Tell me!"

With a sigh the datu rose to his feet and walked across to the carved wooden staff stuck in the ground at the central point of the diagram. Grasping it firmly he pulled up the staff and laid it on the ground. He took the dead cock which lay waiting, and with slow, deliberate movements he wiped out each line he had drawn. Ginjang's heart pounded and his chest tightened as he watched and waited.

[1]See Glossary for meaning of Indonesian words.

The datu took his seat again on the rattan mat. Priest, prophet, healer, he too had authority, of a different order from that of a raja. He looked at Ginjang now, and in a stern voice, with full authority, he spoke.

"This child must die."

"Die?"

The datu gestured to his book, his staff, to the ground before them.

"The spirits of the ancestors, the eight points of the compass, all the gods say the same thing. If this child lives, your kingdom will be overthrown and the very foundations of Batak tradition, our adat, will be destroyed. He will lead our people astray into a strange new teaching."

The blood drained from Ginjang's face as he stared at the datu.

"For your own sake, for your kingdom, and for the sake of adat, of Batak tradition, you must kill this baby at once. Throw it in the river!"

Gathering up his book, his calendar and his staff, the datu rose majestically, and with a curt nod he departed.

Ginjang sat like a stone.

Do the spirits lie?

There had been rumours before, he knew, of a strange teaching with power to destroy kingdoms. Thirty years ago, before Ginjang was born, two white men had appeared in the Silindung valley. In faltering Batak they brought a message of good news about their king, Jesus Christ: "Your kingdoms must become small, like little children, so that the kingdom of Jesus can come." The Batak chieftains listened politely, but what was good news to the Englishmen sounded like very bad news to them. Courage and strength and virility were a Batak's most essential virtues. How could they ever be received in the Kingdom of the Dead if they became weak and childlike? So they nodded respectfully, and feasted their visitors, and sent them away.

But that was not the end of it. Shortly afterwards a great

warlord from the south had swept through the whole area, burning down villages, killing the men, and carrying off young girls
and cattle. The Bataks fled for their lives to the jungle until the
ravagers had gone. As they crept out again in their ones and twos,
to rebuild their devastated homes and fields, the rajas nodded
solemnly to one another. "It's all happened just as those white
men said it would!" they whispered. And with hatred in their
hearts they determined never again to allow white men to invade
their territory.

So the next two westerners who came to Silundung, ten years
later, were killed and eaten.

Now here was the threat of dangerous teaching coming from
the Batak people themselves: from Ginjang's own son. He had
prayed to the ancestors for a promise, and been given a curse.
With a weak step and heavy heart, the raja climbed the short
ladder to his house.

It was an imposing structure from the outside, like all old Batak
houses. Standing firmly on solid piles about a metre high, it had
richly carved wooden walls of black, red and white, and a high,
saddleshaped, fibre roof rising to formidable points adorned with
baffalo horns. The inside was more like a black, smoke-filled
cavern than anything else. Coming up the steps from underneath
the house, Ginjang gasped for breath, as always, as the acrid fumes
of frying chillies caught at his throat.

At the near end of the long central fireplace his second wife
squatted by the wood fire, stirring briskly and talking all the while
in a low murmur. He looked beyond her to the still form of his
first wife, who lay roasting her back against the larger, sacred fire
of childbirth, with the tiny creature of doom at her breast. What
was the mother's name? Risma, was it? The personal, private
name was used so rarely that now, when he wanted to be gentle,
he could not remember it. Boru Hutabarat, daughter of the
Hutabarat clan, stiffened suddenly as she stared across at him,
but her face was in darkness and he could not see the black eyes

which widened in fear. His own face was lit up by the dancing flames, and she saw written plainly there the horror and the dread as he looked at her and her baby.

Ginjang sat down heavily at the top of the steps and recounted in awesome detail all that the datu had said. His younger wife, Boru Manik, set down her cooking pots and edged closer to her sister. Boru Hutabarat said nothing. She could only lie there, cursing her fate, screaming out in her heart to the gods and spirits, asking them why, why — what had she done that they should hate her so much?

There was a long silence. Ginjang cleared his throat. "The child is cursed," he said gruffly.

As if in answer the baby stirred and whimpered, and his mother gently shifted him to the other breast. She knew without a doubt that if the raja's own wellbeing and the safety of his kingdom were threatened, then her baby would surely be sacrificed.

But was there no way out? The raja sat there still, lost in thought. Another man might have plucked the baby from her and cast him down instantly against the stone hearth, or carried him off in anger and hurled him into the river. Ginjang sat there, and every minute that passed was a gain for herself and her child.

"We could go away?" she murmured eventually.

Her husband nodded. "Maybe," he said.

Two days later, when she had recovered her strength, the daughter of the Hutabarats fastened her baby in a sling, and took her older son and her daughter by the hand. Her husband walked with her to the entrance of the village, and stood watching as the little group made its way down the track. Three servants went with them as escorts, to carry their belongings and protect them from danger. Perhaps they were sent also to explain to the Hutabarat clan that this was no disgrace to be avenged. Their daughter was being returned to them with all care and attention, because of an augury that could not be ignored.

Ginjang watched them out of sight, then turned back and looked at his village, Saitnihuta, with its two rows of houses and the open square in the middle where the fearful prediction had been given. He rested his hand for reassurance on the strong earthen wall, which was topped by a thicket of prickly bamboo, a green ring of protection towering up to enclose and shelter his territory. These defences would not easily be broken.

Some chickens were scratching away at the ground by his house. His one remaining son came trotting out and laughed as they scattered, then looked about him vacantly, at a loss now his playmates had gone. Well, his mother was young and strong. There would be more sons. Ginjang gnawed at his lip as he walked back across the square, wondering if he had done the right thing, the wise thing; hoping he had not been weak and foolish.

And so the baby was allowed to live.

THE STRANGE NEW TEACHING 1

I ngwar Ludwig Nommensen shielded his eyes from the sun's glare as he gazed down at the Silindung valley, spread out before him in a vast expanse of shimmering green and gold and brown. Dotted here and there among the ricefields were thick round clumps of trees, sticking out like tufts of wool on a patchwork quilt. Each one, he knew, marked a Batak village. Nommensen sank to his knees on the coarse, springy grass of the mountain top.

"Dear Lord," he prayed, "Whether I live or die, I will make my home here, among these people you died to redeem, and I shall proclaim your gospel here."

The German missionary had first heard of Silindung seventeen years before, when he was twelve years old. A collision with a horse and carriage had put him in bed for a year, with a crushed leg which refused to heal. Doggedly he practised his arithmetic, and pored over the family's one book, the Bible. His friends repeated to him their teacher's stories of missionary journeys to distant lands, and of two Americans killed by the Bataks of Sumatra in 1834.

"The very year I was born," breathed Ludwig. It seemed hugely significant.

Then came the doctor's decision to amputate the leg. Ludwig had been reading the promise of Jesus in John 16:23, that "My Father will give you whatever you ask in my name." Might these words still apply today? He asked his mother, and she assured him that they did. With an obscure feeling that he should offer something in return, the boy vowed that if God healed his leg, he would take the gospel to the spirit-worshippers of Sumatra. Six weeks later he was fully recovered. From that time onwards he worked steadily towards his goal.

Difficulties abounded. Ludwig's family was poor, and after his father's death in 1848 he had to work hard to support his mother and sisters. For five years he tended cows and sheep, and worked on building projects, until his mother was ready for him to leave. Then, with a Bible, hymnbook and catechism, and a small bundle of clothes, he set off for the port where his uncle lived.

He intended to work his passage on an ocean-going ship, and thus reach his missionfield. But the Lord had other plans. Nommensen tried for six months to get a job on a ship, but with no success. Through a meeting with his old teacher, however, he obtained a position as an apprentice teacher, and the opportunity to study. Eventually he was able to train at the theological school at Barmen; and in 1861 he was ordained and sent out as a missionary by the Rhenish Mission Society.

Nommensen landed at Padang, on the west coast of Sumatra, in May 1862. He spent some months on the coast, learning Batak and the commonly used Malay (later to become the Indonesian national language). At the end of the year he moved inland to Sipirok, to join the small group of missionaries who had recently begun work among the Bataks. He longed to press on northwards to Silindung, but his colleagues had decided to concentrate on the southern part of the Batak Highlands, the only part under Dutch control. The Dutch authorities were unwilling for missionaries to work where they had no influence. In any case the Silindung valley was disrupted at that time by fighting between rival Batak clans.

In 1863, however, missionaries travelled through Silindung and made contact with a friendly and powerful chieftain, Raja Pontas Lumbantobing. Their report of the trip convinced Nommensen that the time was right. He set off on November 7, 1863, with two helpers to carry the basic essentials and two Batak guides to show the way.

It was the fifth day of their journey when Nommensen first saw his goal. They had been climbing since dawn, following a twisting, tortuous track that meandered between the ricefields or beside ambling streams, then teetered along cliff edges or broke off suddenly to strike upwards through patches of dense forest. They walked in single file with Nommensen in the middle. High overhead the trees met in a leafy ceiling, and all about them the undergrowth was thick with sounds. More than once the man in front stopped, put up a hand for silence, darted forward, smashed the head of a snake with his stick, and walked on without a word. Then suddenly they emerged from darkness into light — a wide grassy slope spattered with curling green ferns and yellow flowers, under a silvery blue sky. As Nommensen strode on up the mountainside his heart sang. And there, far below him, stretched mile upon mile of lush green ricefields.

"Silindung valley," murmured the guide.

"We'll rest here for an hour or so before we go down," said Nommensen.

The trek downhill seemed quicker and easier. They passed through a small market town on the lower slopes, picking up a gaggle of young lads who trailed along behind them, hissing insults from a safe distance.

"Yah, goat's eyes!"

"Where yn' going, Dutchman?"

"Go home Mister!"

"Hss! Hss! Rat's baby!"

Nommensen's helper turned swiftly as one of the boys made a grab at the baggage.

"Hss yourself! Go away!" he snarled.

Nommensen shook his head and turned to the lad with a smile and an outstretched hand.

"Where do you live, boy?" he asked.

But the crowd had already scattered, to creep back later and follow at a distance again.

They were on the flat now, making their way between the rice-fields. A man sat dozing in his shelter beside the track. He roused himself as the procession drew near, and jumped down to see what was happening.

"Where are you going, sir?" he called in Malay, with a smile for Nommensen and a curt gesture with his hand to shoo away the unwelcome entourage.

"We're making our way to Saitnihuta, Ompu," said Nommensen. "Is it far now?"

"I can show you, sir," said the Batak, tugging the cloth of his sarung more firmly round his hips, and waving his arms again to get rid of the youths. "Ompu Tarida," he introduced himself. "I'll come with you." He set off eagerly along the track.

The floor of the valley seemed to be one vast expanse of paddyfields, broken up by the many villages each hidden behind its strong earthen wall topped by high bamboo thickets. The fortified villages were called lumban, the Batak explained, and a group of lumban made a huta. Saitnihuta was the name of a district, but it could also refer to the central village, the bagasan, where the chief raja lived.

"Huta means town," he told Nommensen, "And sait — well, that's that sharp tooth, dog tooth, that sticks down — sharp and fierce! So the people of Saitnihuta are very cruel, very fierce. You'll see."

It was late afternoon when they reached the village of Saitnihuta. Watchmen gave the alarm as they approached, and the raja came forward to meet them. He stared through narrowed eyes at the slight, pale-skinned young man with the watery-blue eyes and long nose.

"My name is Nommensen," said the missionary. "My friends have visited your valley in the company of Raja Pontas."

"My uncle," said the raja cautiously. He straightened his shoulders and introduced himself. "Ompu Ginjang Lumbantobing. Son of Sumuntul."

He nodded towards the sopo, where the young men of the village slept. This large wooden building also did duty as guest house, council chamber and rice barn. A servant showed Nommensen's helpers where to stow their belongings, while another rolled out a mat on the floor. Ginjang motioned for Nommensen and Tarida to sit down beside him. With a flourish the missionary handed over the presents he had brought: a sarung for the raja, and tobacco. The men of the village took a hunk each and pressed it down into the bowls of their long copper pipes as they found their places on the floor. The low rumble of voices was pierced suddenly by sharp squeals of terror, high and urgent.

"A pig is being killed," murmured the raja. They would eat well that night.

As they waited, the men interrogated Nommensen.

"Why have you come here?"

"The Company sent you, didn't they, to spy out the land, so that the Dutch can come and conquer us!"

"No, I'm not employed by the Dutch East India Company," said Nommensen. "I'm not interested in colonizing your country. I'm a missionary. A pendeta. I want to tell you some good news about God."

Ginjang grunted, but said nothing.

"I want to live here, in this valley." Nommensen smiled round at the scowling faces. "Build a house and a school. I shall teach everyone who wants to be clever and happy."

"You can't build a house here," said one of the men. "We'll burn it down."

"Then I shall build another."

"We don't need a school here. We're clever enough already."

"We know you want to steal our children and send them away to be slaves for the white men."

"We'll cut off his thick white thigh," muttered an older man in Batak, "and roast it for dinner."

Nommensen stiffened slightly, and Ginjang realized that he understood the local language. Until then they had been using the more widely spoken Malay.

The missionary reached for his harmonica, and began to play. The Bataks listened, enthralled. They loved music. Soon they were swaying in time to his playing. There were shouts of surprise when he suddenly picked out a Batak tune he had learned in Sipirok. Some of the young men rushed to fetch their own instruments, and soon they too took up the melody with their simple flutes and two-stringed lutes. Then Nommensen sang for them, a simple hymn, first in German and then the first verse again in his own Batak translation. By the time the meal was ready everyone was feeling much more friendly, and even Ginjang relaxed a little.

After a special meal of pork, cooked in its own blood, the questioning began again.

"How many children do you have?"

"I'm not married yet," said Nommensen, aware that the admission made him less than adult in Batak thinking. "But my fiancée will join me here when I have a house ready for her." He turned to the raja. "How many children have you, Ompu?"

It was Ginjang's turn to stiffen. "Enough," he said gruffly, after a pause. "Enough."

Later that night, as they prepared to sleep on the hard benches of the sopo, the village boys told Nommensen about the augury, and how the raja had banished his wife and children forever, to save the whole kingdom from a terrible curse.

"A strange and dangerous teaching," Nommensen repeated to himself as he twisted about, trying to find a less uncomfortable position. Ants were exploring his legs, and he was uneasily conscious of something larger rustling by his head. To think that a man could turn out his wife and children on the strength of a datu's prediction! As his eyes closed he seemed to see the massive grey stone walls of an impregnable fortress, the binding power of evil spirits, enclosing the Batak people. How could he begin to reach them?

He remembered the verse he had read from Samuel that morning: "Nothing can hinder the Lord from saving, whether by many or by few." Those walls could and would be broken, he was sure. But it would need endless patience, and a strength and love that only God could give.

Nommensen stayed on for a while in Saitnihuta. He went with the villagers to the nearby market, and strolled round, making friends with the children and meeting all the local rajas. Soon he was a familiar figure there, with his gentle, slightly lopsided smile, and the quietly determined set of his narrow shoulders. He carried a stick, to ward off dogs and pigs; and the locals, who had their own beliefs about sticks, kept a wary distance. His eyes flashed under their thick brows when he found someone being cruel. When fights broke out, which they did every day, he brought out his medicine box to tend the wounded, telling them all the while of the loving God who desired peace among men. He told them again of his desire to build a house in Silindung, and they repeated their threats to burn it down.

One day a deputation went to see Raja Ginjang.

"We don't like this foreigner," they told him. "His words sound sweet enough but his heart may be different."

"I know," said Ginjang. Nommensen posed a threat, he was sure, to their whole way of life. But Raja Pontas had welcomed the missionaries, had given them his sanction, as it were. And Raja Pontas was Ginjang's uncle, who must be respected, besides being one of the most powerful men in Silindung valley.

That afternoon Ginjang spoke with Nommensen.

"You must leave my sopo tomorrow."

"Oh?"

"Yes," said the raja. "It's almost harvest time. See my ricefields?

I'll be harvesting the paddy soon, and then I'll need to store it in the sopo. You won't be able to sleep there then."

Nommensen bowed stiffly. "I wouldn't want to cause you any inconvenience."

"You must go tomorrow."

Nommensen moved out the next day. He found shelter for a few nights in a neighbouring village, then had to move again, with the same reason given. He was looking for land to build on, but no one would sell. He smiled and shrugged and kept on asking.

Raja Pontas arrived at Ginjang's house one day in a towering rage, complaining loudly that the missionary had been lost to their enemy. The Sumurung, a rival branch of the same Lumbantobing clan, had invited him to stay with them. Eventually it was agreed that Nommensen could build his house on a piece of marshland between Sumuntul and Sumurung territory, where the river had run past Saitnihuta village until a recent earth tremor changed its course.

Even then Nommensen had the greatest difficulty in gathering together the wood he needed, most of which had to be taken from an abandoned building. Constant threats and interruptions accompanied the building work, but Nommensen and his helpers pressed on. Finally they succeeded in building a house, and later a school and church on the same compound.

In September 1864 a great feast was called, to honour an ancestor spirit. Ompu Tarida, Nommensen's first friend in Silindung, came to warn him.

"You must keep away, Ompu," he said. "We all know that *you* are to be the sacrifice!"

"Your people can't harm one hair of my head unless the Lord allows it," said Nommensen slowly, remembering the two who had been murdered thirty years before. "I think I must attend the feast."

"But you'll be killed!"

The feast day came, and the Bataks gathered in their

thousands. With much ceremony a waterbuffalo was led in and tied to a stake in the middle of the square. The datu and the spirit medium danced majestically before their ancestor, with offerings of rice and fish, and much drinking of palm wine. The rajas danced, and then the women, then the men again. Louder and louder pounded the gongs and drums.

Suddenly the medium screamed out in a frenzy. "My grandchildren! This foreigner wants to burn down my home! Don't you care? You insult me with this buffalo! But beware! I won't bless you unless you kill a man for me, in the true Batak way!"

Nommensen stood up. "This can't possibly be your ancestor speaking," he said calmly. "For what grandmother could urge her grandchildren to fight and kill one another? Surely Satan must be deceiving you!"

The Bataks stared aghast at Nommensen's effrontery. The chief raja lunged his spear into the buffalo's flesh, meaning to kill it instantly. But he missed the heart, and the crowd watched in a tense silence as he wrestled with the animal for half an hour before it dropped dead. Suddenly the skies opened and a torrential deluge thundered down to put an end to the feast. Nommensen walked home unharmed.

A year later he baptized his first converts; eight adults (including Ompu Tarida) and five children. All were expelled from their villages as traitors to adat, the Batak traditions, and their lands were seized because they would no longer contribute towards ceremonies asking the spirits to bless the crops. Nommensen took them in. Gradually his settlement extended to become a village, as more and more Christians sought refuge there. They named it Huta Dame: Peace Town.

In 1866 Nommensen's bride came to join him, escorted from Germany by a new young missionary, Johannsen. First Raja Pontas, and then the other rajas, feasted the newly-weds in turn. They watched in fascination as the young white woman unwrapped her plate, knife, fork and spoon and ate in the western manner. Some of them grappled, for a while, with the new implements, but soon abandoned them in favour of fingers and banana leaves.

People flocked to Huta Dame from all around, for medical help, or schooling, or for advice in settling disputes. Soon there were so many Christians in Silindung valley that new believers did not need to flee from their villages. The strange new teaching was becoming acceptable.

As new students came to the school, Nommensen recorded the name and village of each one, and checked that his parents agreed to his enrollment. His attention was caught by one young teenager who came to register in 1870.

"What's your family name?" he asked, as usual.

"Lumbantobing."

"Village?"

"I come from the Hutabarat district," said the boy, naming a village.

Nommensen looked up, surprised. He knew enough about the clan system by now to realize that a Lumbantobing from a Hutabarat village was rare indeed.

"Very well," he nodded, "I am happy to welcome you to my school."

Stirring at the back of his mind was a memory of the raja at Saitnihuta who had banished his newborn son because of a datu's warning. Could this be the one?

Nommensen said nothing, but he watched the new boy carefully. He was a bright student, keen to grapple with the mysteries of reading and writing, ready to join in the physical tasks of farming, listening with rapt attention to the Bible stories and the simple message of salvation. He was baptized with the name Cleopas.

"IF THIS CHILD LIVES ... " 2

"**I**'ve come to invite you to the baptism service."

Raja Ginjang looked at his uncle in amazement.

"Next Sunday I shall be baptized, with my wife and children."

Ginjang's head was spinning. He knew, of course, that Ompu Pontas had welcomed the missionaries to Silindung, and had even encouraged his people to attend Nommensen's school. He saw the new education as a door to progress and material benefit. By contrast the great Batak leader of the Lake Toba region, Sisingamangaraja, opposed not only Dutch imperialism but all things western. Pontas had helped Nommensen unobtrusively with gifts of rice and vegetables, and his sanction had done much to create a more peaceful situation in which Bataks could acknowledge the Christian faith without fear of reprisals.

But a raja was the keeper of adat, whose position in society was divinely appointed by the ancestor spirits and minutely defined according to the intricate rulings of Batak tradition. For such a man *himself* to become a Christian...!

"Pendeta Nommensen has been coming to my house each day to teach me the Christian religion, and now I am ready to confess my faith," Pontas continued to explain.

"Your faith?"

"To say that I believe in Jesus Christ." Pontas laughed. "You do well to look surprised — I've been long enough about it! But it started a long time back. When I was a child, maybe, and those first white men came here and told us about the Kingdom of God."

Ginjang stirred uneasily. He had heard that story many times.

"I didn't understand it then, of course," mused Pontas. "But I never forgot them." He stabbed the air with an expressive finger. "And then when Nommensen came, well ... I watched him."

"We all did."

"He seemed so friendly and kind ... Tough too," the raja added. "Do you remember how we threatened to kill him?"

Ginjang nodded.

"I told him a proverb, remember. 'If you throw down some grains of rice on the path,' I said, 'then of course the birds will come and peck them up.' And he said yes, they would, but if you keep driving the birds away, then they won't get a chance to pick up the rice." Pontas chuckled. "He was so sure that his God would protect him. And that's what happened. If we pulled his house down, he'd build it up again. Threats didn't scare him away! Poison couldn't get rid of him!"

"My cousin tried it," said Ginjang. "Went to the house very early when the helper was cooking porridge. Stirred in some strong poison when the boy wasn't looking. But the missionary ate the porridge and never even felt sick!"

"The dog did though! Nommensen's great black dog came bounding up to eat the scraps, and promptly fell writhing on the ground and died!" Pontas paused. "Ompu Nommensen knew what had happened all right. But he just kept on talking about peace and forgiveness and Jesus Christ. That's why your cousin admitted what he'd done and became a Christian. And now I'm a Christian too. I'm going to be baptized on Sunday and I'm changing my name to Obaya: Servant of God."

"*Servant* of God?" Ginjang could hardly believe his ears. Fundamental to a Batak was his sense of status. Wars had been fought because at a feast a man was offered a more lowly part of the pig's anatomy than his rank required. Rajas were rajas and slaves were slaves. Even the spirits were appeased and manipulated — and often deceived — for what they could give in the way of material benefits, rather than from any sense that reverence was their due. Never were they *served*. But now the most feared and respected raja in the whole Silindung valley was about to take the name *Servant* of God.

"You'll come to the service, then?" said Raja Pontas as he rose to leave.

"Yes, Ompu, I shall come with my family." What else could he do?

Raja Pontas was renowned in Silindung, both for his wisdom and knowledge of the customary laws (adat), and for his strict but just dealings with his people. His baptism had a marked effect on the spread of Christianity in the region. If the leading raja embraced the new religion, surely it was no longer to be considered a threat to Batak society and tradition?

The datus complained to Nommensen that the paddy would all be eaten by rats because the Christian women had worked in the fields on the day set aside for special ceremonies to worship the spirits. The missionary summoned a meeting of Christian and non-Christian rajas, to thrash the matter out. Pontas argued that their ancestors were more likely to favour the Christians, who worked hard and did good. In the old days, he added, everyone had joined together to chase away the rats.

"But our ancestors sacrificed to the spirits too," was the reply.

"Yes, I do remember my father dancing before the spirits with a rat on his head," agreed Pontas. "And then he threw it into the river." He shook his head sorrowfully. "It swam across the river, and lived and prospered on the other side." He wagged a finger at the listening crowd. "But just think, my brothers, if the rat had been killed first and then thrown into the river, then we should have had one less rat to contend with now!"

Everyone laughed.

Raja Ginjang listened to such exchanges, and pondered long over all these new happenings. Then one day he himself went to see Nommensen, and asked the missionary to come regularly to his house to teach him about the Christian faith.

Something was happening to Raja Ginjang. Each day he looked forward to Nommensen's visit. He followed closely as the missionary took him through the basic Christian teaching: of God who created the world; of man and of sin; of Jesus Christ and his triumph over death and Satan; of the free gift of salvation and a new life to all who believed and gave their lives to Him. There was something tremendously attractive about this new teaching. Ginjang's heart warmed as he listened to the gospel stories.

But as he studied, the raja was being torn apart. All that he learned accused him. The God whom Nommensen preached demanded obedience and love instead of the easy propitiation of rice and ritual. And the power He gave was different too. Ginjang's old belief in the spirits and their power to win victories — his trust in the datu's power to predict fortunes — all this was false and against God's will. Then what of his own baby son? Every evening the raja paced up and down outside his house pounding a clenched fist against an open palm. He repeated to himself over and over the words of the datu on that fateful day, fifteen years before. He remembered his wife's face as she fastened the baby in its sling and prepared to leave.

Eventually he admitted to Nommensen what he had done. The missionary listened calmly.

"God forgives us *all* our sins," he assured the raja, "no matter how grave, provided we truly repent and confess them." He paused. "But sometimes we need to put things right, too."

"Yes, I want to. But how?"

"You have responsibilities which you have neglected all these years. I think you need to call back your wife and children, and provide for them."

Ginjang nodded.

"But if you want to become a Christian, you need to be clear which wife you are going to live with in a marriage relationship. You know God's plan is for His children to have only one wife each."

"Mmm." Ginjang gnawed at his lip thoughtfully. "I could build a new house, perhaps, for my first wife."

"Good idea."

"I'm building already, as it happens, on some land I got from Sumurung — my spoils from the end of the last war. I want to build another lumban, a fortified village you know, ready for the next lot of fighting." He grinned awkwardly, knowing Nommensen disapproved of warfare. "It's a separate village," he explained, "but very close. Boru Hutabarat could live there with her children. I'll send a message, telling her to get ready to move."

"Very good," said Nommensen, standing up. "I should tell you, by the way, that I think the son you talked about may be a student at my school."

Ginjang was supervising the building work when Nommensen came next, bringing with him a boy about fifteen years old. The raja knew at once who it must be. Very slowly and reluctantly he walked across the open ground to where the visitors stood waiting.

"Good afternoon," he said brusquely. "We're building, you see." He turned away abruptly to point out the men working high above ground. "Come and look."

Nommensen and Cleopas exchanged glances, then turned to follow Ginjang across the square.

Cleopas wiped a clammy palm on his new, Dutch-style trousers as he walked. He had not at all wanted to meet with this man who had once banished him forever. But it was very hard to resist Ompu Nommensen, with his gentle smile and his fatherly words of wisdom. The boy looked with interest at the skeleton of his future home, towering up above him.

"Amazing!" breathed Nommensen, craning his neck to watch the men manoeuvre the heavy central beam for the roof into place, then secure it with swiftly bound rope and a wooden peg. "No nails!"

Ginjang pointed out the massive foundation posts, which had been soaked for weeks in mud to give added strength. They must stand for a hundred years.

At their feet two young Bataks were absorbed in carving elaborate figures on a plank for the front wall, while an older man fashioned a fearsome buffalo head. This was to be the house of a raja's family. Ginjang clearly intended to build a dwelling worthy of his first wife, perhaps as a gesture of regret for the past.

Wood shavings lay all around. Cleopas kicked at them with his toe, then squatted down to run a finger over the spiral motif of the wooden carving. He nodded at the craftsman, a boy of about his own age.

"Very good," he murmured, then looked up awkwardly to meet Raja Ginjang's eyes.

The raja turned away abruptly with a grunt, and led them off on a rapid tour of the new settlement. He was clearly feeling ill at east. Gruffly he pointed out the sopo, and the well, and the huge pile of timber stacked ready to build the next house. He addressed all his comments to Nommensen, ignoring Cleopas, and yet darting quick glances at the boy from time to time, from under frowning brows.

The young student looked and listened respectfully, not noticeably embarrassed by the occasion. (Ginjang could not see the pounding heart.) He was tall for his age, and sturdy, with a clear open face like his mother's and smiling brown eyes.

"If this child lives, your kingdom will be overthrown and the very foundations of Batak tradition, our adat, will be destroyed. He will lead our people astray into a strange new teaching."

What was it the missionary had said, about God loving His children? And about love casting out fear?

"He will lead our people astray into a strange new teaching."

As he watched Cleopas, the raja repeated to himself the datu's prediction. Suddenly Nommensen turned to ask him a question, and like a thunderbolt came the realization that he himself,

Ginjang Lumbantobing, had already accepted the new teaching and found it good! He was preparing for baptism. He had his new name ready chosen: Solomon. A great and wise king, the missionary had told him. And how he needed wisdom now!

Ginjang stopped and held out his hand. He blinked hard.

"You are my son," he said.

Cleopas looked into his father's eyes; the father he had walked and talked with so often in day dreams, whose vengeance he had fled from in nightmares. He smiled.

With the major hurdle over, the family was soon able to move into the new village, which was named Pulopulo II. As well as Cleopas, his mother, brother and sister, Ginjang sent a number of other families to live there too, with strict orders to build up the fortifications and guard it well. The thick clay-brick wall, with its narrow, tunnel-like entrance, was planted on top with prickly bamboo and thorn bushes. In time this would provide a strong protection. As yet however it was far from perfect.

For already they were at war. In a new burst of fighting, the leaders of Sumurung's army had all been killed. There was no doubt that he would seek revenge. Nommensen worked tirelessly to bring the two sides together in peace, reminding them that warfare meant murder and was against God's will. Raja Ginjang, newly baptized now with the name Solomon, shrugged his shoulders helplessly and marshalled his defences.

On a still, moonless night, Cleopas and his brother Moses took their turn to guard the wall at Pulopulo II. They sat in silence on top of the wall, watching and waiting, guns at the ready, eyes and ears straining to detect the slightest movement in the thick blackness that covered them. Nothing stirred. Not a star shone. The hours passed slowly, and Cleopas shivered as he drew his blanket more tightly round his shoulders. His head grew heavy, jerked up once, then sank slowly on his chest. He slept. Moses crouched beside him, listening. But the night lingered too long about her business, and he too fell asleep.

Towards dawn a solitary figure approached the wall from outside and began to climb. First a hand, then a knee, and he was
just about to stand upright on the wall when an ear-shattering
howl jerked him off balance. A huge dog bounded up, barking
furiously.

"Wake up! Wake up!" yelled a woman's voice from the
nearest house, as the dog's owner shook her husband firmly by
the shoulder. "What's happening? The dog's barking!"

With a snarl of rage, the intruder kicked out at the dog. "Shut
up, you stupid bitch!"

Jolted out of oblivion, the two brothers started up. Moses caught
at his brother's arm to signal the need for quiet as they peered
through the darkness. There was a soft thud as their enemy hit
the ground, then plunged off into the gloom. Moses grabbed his
rifle and fired blindly in the general direction of the noise.

"Quick!" He leaped off the wall, with Cleopas hard on his heels.

Men and boys were pouring out of the houses, snatching up
guns and knives and clubs as they came, yelling and shouting,
determined to see blood shed.

"That way! He went off that way!"

"Over here! After him!"

Waving their weapons aloft, and threatening vengeance on any
who dared to attack their village, they hurtled through the undergrowth. But it was too late.

"He's gone." Moses put his arm round his brother's shoulder
and turned to face the excited crowd. "We lost him."

Disappointed, they walked home together in the quickening dawn,
making eager plans for a better watch on future nights, and specu-
lating as to why one man should scale the wall alone instead of
attacking with an army.

A few days later one of the women of the village set off to the
market to buy rice. A tall, broadshouldered young man with just
the beginnings of a paunch was sauntering down the road towards
her, a cousin on her father's side who she realized must be the

new commander of Sumurung's army. He caught her arm as she went by.

"Tell me, Aunt." he asked politely. "Who was on guard the other night, on your village wall?"

"When do you mean? Why do you want to know?"

"There was a dog barking — made so much noise we could hear over in our village, even. What was all the row about? What was the matter?"

She looked at him for a moment, exasperated and a little afraid. She hated this never-ending warfare between members of the same clan.

"Oh well," she began with a sigh, wondering just how much of the story he knew already. "It was my dog barking, if you must know, and it woke us all up because someone was trying to climb over the wall. And I'm very glad it did, because whoever it was, he fell off the wall and ran away, head over heels." She dropped her voice, "And if it hadn't been for that..."

"Well?"

"Right by the place where he was climbing was where the watchmen had fallen asleep! Two brothers who are very dear to us."

"Two brothers?"

"Raja Ginjang's two sons, Moses and Cleopas. Raja Solomon, I should say," she corrected herself.

"Oh, by all the gods and spirits!" The commander smacked his forehead with his fist and stamped his feet in a rage. "Would you believe it! They were my chief target that night!" He glowered at her and shook his fist. "If only that dog of yours had kept quiet! If I'd got *one* of their heads, even, I'd have had a big reward from Ompu Sumurung!"

The woman stared at him wide-eyed, then turned on her heel and hurried home, to tell her neighbours all she had heard.

Nommensen, meanwhile, was still trying to reconcile the two sides, and persuade his noble converts that constant warfare was contrary to God's will for Christians. In any case they were weary of all the fighting and only needed a way of saving face. When Raja Pontas stepped in as arbitrator, and summoned a special peace feast according to adat, there was general agreement. A buffalo was slaughtered, and two pigs. The Bataks ate their fill. They sang and danced, and made long speeches with promises of peace and friendship and goodwill. No need to mention past conflicts and who might or might not have been to blame.

So Ginjang's son Cleopas, after his second narrow escape from death, was free to continue his studies at Nommensen's school.

THE DISCIPLE 3

Nommensen's teaching methods were straightforward. He saw many needs in Batak society, and tried to prepare his students to meet them. Besides literacy and a thorough grounding in the Bible, he taught practical subjects such as health, hygiene and agriculture.

When he taught medicine, the students shared in caring for the sick. They learned to diagnose and deal with common ailments such as the everyday cuts and wounds, the fevers and diarrhoea. Nommensen showed them how to make simple medicines from the plants growing nearby, and what quantities to use. They must always pray first, he said: medicine was a tool, but God alone had power to heal.

When he taught farming methods, Nommensen worked in the paddyfields alongside his students. They drained the marshland, prepared the ground, laid out irrigation channels, planted the seed, harvested the rice. Any implements that were needed they made themselves.

Cloopas watched in amasement. In his society the rajas grew their fingernails long, to show they had no need to work in the fields. But here was a man — not a raja, it was true, but a man with the same white skin as the Dutch lords — wading through the mud beside him and breaking his back under the scorching sun, just to show him the best way to transplant young rice shoots.

Nommensen gave his gentle smile, his head a little on one side to offset the deafness in one ear, and held out a juicy green shoot.

"Do you see now?" he asked.

"Yes," said Cleopas. He saw a lot.

Patient yet firm, as teacher, leader, counsellor, friend, Nommensen had a gift for disciple-making. And Cleopas had never before had a father he could look up to.

For his own part, Nommensen had ambitions for his Batak students that were far ahead of his time.

"How do you think our Mission views gifted nationals?" he wrote to the board in Germany. "There are people here in Silindung valley who have real ability as catechists, through the grace of the Lord Jesus. In time they should be able to do more than we can. It would be very much cheaper, in my opinion, to use these workers than to rely on missionaries from Europe to do everything. Besides which, they will surely be much better able to probe the hearts and to understand the mindset of their own people, if only we can teach them and prepare them well. That's why I beg of you to send out more workers who can teach them ...

"One day this nation will surely be independent. Then they will train and appoint their own teachers and ministers, as we do in other lands."

Nommensen's aim was to set up a middle school to train the older students as evangelists and lay church workers. One had been established in Sipirok, in the southern part of Batakland, in 1868, and in five years it had already provided 27 graduates to work as assistants to the Dutch and German missionaries. Unfortunately both the missionaries in charge of the school had had to return to Europe because of ill health. Nommensen longed to start a new school of the same standard in Silindung.

The Bataks were spiritually hungry — they were coming in their droves for Christian teaching, far faster than teachers could be found for them. Further south it seemed that Islam was establishing itself just as rapidly. It was vital to seize the harvest while they could. But how could workers be trained? Manpower was short and Nommensen himself already had a heavy workload.

Nommensen discussed the problem with his two young colleagues in Silindung, Johannsen and Mohri. Both were heavily committed to their newly established congregations: Johannsen at Pansur Napitu, and Mohri at Sipoholon. But between them they hit on a solution. Rather than moving the teachers to a central school building, why not move the school itself from centre to centre?

Thus was born the idea of the travelling school. The thirty graduates from Nommensen's elementary school were invited to become the first intake. The students would rotate, spending a month with each teacher before moving on to the next. The school opened in 1875, and Cleopas, the oldest at nineteen, was elected head student.

Nommensen had now moved from Huta Dame. The lowlying swampland, once a riverbed, was subject to constant flooding and had proved a serious health hazard. After Nommensen himself was ill for several months his colleagues insisted on a move. Raja Pontas and Raja Solomon (Ginjang) between them provided a piece of land on the hillside at Pearaja, overlooking Nommensen's earlier home. Before the new buildings were finished, however, his eldest daughter died. His wife too fell sick. She had to be carried uphill on a stretcher, and in fact she never completely recovered, but always walked with a stick thereafter.

So it was at Pearaja the students gathered for their first month's schooling, bringing with them a month's supply of rice and other essentials. Nommensen taught them how to preach, and also basic physics, medicine and German. After a week's holiday the second month would be spent with Johannsen at Pansur Napitu, studying geography, sociology, mathematics, pastoral care and the catechism. In the third month they learned Malay, Islamics, music and church administration.

Travel could be dangerous in those days. There was constant warfare between clans and villages, and a passing stranger might easily be taken for an enemy. Because of this, Nommensen insisted that they assemble at Pearaja at the start of each monthly term, so that they could walk as a group to the next study centre.

"Be careful how you go," he reminded Cleopas, as they prepared to set out for their second month at Pansur Napitu eight
kilometres away. "There's a war on again, between Pansur Napitu
and the Sitompul clan. You don't want to get involved."

"No, of course not," agreed Cleopas.

"Remember, a soft word turns away wrath."

Cleopas grinned. "We know what to say, sir."

Nommensen looked round the group with a stern eye. "Don't
forget you are Christians. You won't flare up if someone insults
you, because Jesus Christ is the bringer of peace."

"Yes, Pendeta Nommensen."

The students murmured their agreement as they gathered together their belongings: ten kilos of rice each along with their clothes
and other items.

As they reached the turning for Pansur Napitu, Cleopas slowed
his pace, scanning the countryside with a wary eye open for places
where men might be hiding in ambush. The midday sun was hot,
and some of the younger boys at the back were dragging their
feet.

"We should stop and eat soon," murmured one of the group.

"Ye-es," said Cleopas absently, his eyes still darting from side
to side as he walked. The air was so still it made him catch his
breath ... almost as if ...

"Excuse us!" he called out. "Let us pass through safely please.
We're students and we're on our way to study!"

A clump of thick bushes suddenly parted, and three men stood
blocking the road; heavily-built Bataks, with large knives in their
hands. They stared at the school party without speaking. From
nowhere, it seemed, a crowd appeared behind them.

"We're on our way to study," repeated Cleopas, "Let us pass by
please, Ompu."

It was a well-established custom, in this land of continual strife,
for passersby to call out their names and business as they walked

through a war zone, so that everyone would realize they were neutrals. But this did not always guarantee their safety.

"Where are you going, then, to ...er ..." The Batak eyed them up and down, his gaze lingering on the packs they carried. "To study?" He sneered his contempt for western teaching.

"To Pansur Napitu, Ompu."

A mistake. For these were surely Sitompuls. One of them spat, expressively, at the ground by Cleopas's feet. Sitompuls, certainly, and haters of missionaries it seemed too.

"You're children of that Goat's Eyes, aren't you?" said the man, with sudden understanding.

"Dutch brats! Dutch brats!" One of the children in the crowd started the chant, and another took it up, and then another. Cleopas clenched and unclenched his fists, telling himself to be calm, be patient, think of his teacher.

"Who are you calling Dutch brat?" Joshua had stepped out and grabbed one of the boys by the arm, shaking him hard. "You just stop that, you hear!"

"Joshua!" Cleopas caught his arm. "Remember!"

The three men stepped forward too, knives glinting in the sun.

"Mmm. Yes," said Joshua, letting go abruptly. He stood glowering at the children.

"We don't want to take any part in the fighting," said Cleopas, with as calm a smile as he could manage. "We want to learn all we can so that we can help our own people in every possible way." He swallowed. "We believe that God wants us all to live at peace together."

"Hmmph!" The man snorted, but he put his knife away, and waved an impatient hand to urge them on their way.

"Thank you Ompu," said Cleopas with a nod as he walked on.

"Thank you, Ompu."

"Good day, Ompu."

They all nodded and bowed as they passed by, then walked on in silence until they rounded the next bend in the road. Then they flung down their baggage and went wild; turning cartwheels, throwing sticks, stones, and jackets up into the air, hooting and yelling, and collapsing in giggles on the grass.

"Will somebody tell me just why we put up with it?" said Joshua as he unwrapped his banana leaf and shovelled a handful of sticky rice into his mouth. "Why don't we just fight back?"

"Yes, why not! There were more of us than them, I'm sure — a lot more. We could have taught them a thing or two!"

"Well, you never know," said one of the younger boys doubtfully. "In a place like that, they could have had a whole army, hidden out of sight somewhere."

"If there's one thing I won't stand for, it's being called a Dutch brat!"

Everyone was talking at once.

"It's annoying, I agree," said Cleopas, when the others had said their fill. "But this is the way we have to do it." He looked round at his friends. "That's the way Ompu Nommensen wants it, and that's the way Jesus Christ did it. Agreed?"

They nodded reluctantly.

"But it's hard, though. I get so mad in here, I could burst." Joshua thumped his chest expressively. "And I just want to throttle them!"

"Yes, it is hard," said Cleopas. "But I think I'm coming to see what Ompu Nommensen means. It's when we show them that Jesus is peace-loving that we begin to get the victory over the hate. There'll never be peace here if we fight back all the time. Don't you think so?"

"Yes. Maybe."

The travelling school continued for a year, and then suddenly was forced to close, when a cholera epidemic swept through the Silindung valley. Whole families were wiped out in days as one after another fell sick, until in some villages there were scarcely enough people with the strength to bury their dead.

The datus, whose influence as spiritual leaders had recently eroded, were quick to see signs of judgment. The spirits were angry, they cried, and no wonder, with so many hundreds of their Batak grandchildren deserting them to become Christians! The old sacrifices must be revived at once. Special feasts must be held, and food offered again to the ancestor spirits. But all was to no avail. Magic potions were distributed to the sick, but they died just as quickly. A feeling of gloom engulfed the whole valley.

The Christian students were all sent home to their villages, with what medical supplies could be spared. They worked alongside the missionaries, using their newfound skills in tireless efforts to care for the sick and the dying. The task seemed overwhelming. Hundreds lost their lives. Nommensen himself, his wife and five children came down with the disease, but all recovered. And it was noticeable that the Christian villages suffered less than their animistic neighbours.

Cleopas was at his home in Pulopulo II, mixing a rehydration drink of water, sugar and salt for a neighbour, when a messenger came to tell him his father wanted to see him. He went at once to Saitnihuta.

"I've been thinking," said Ginjang, without any preamble. "You're old enough now. You must be about twenty, is it? And it's time you were choosing a wife."

Cleopas was taken aback. He had not once thought of marriage. His mind had been full of his studies until recently, and now he faced death as a constant reality. Talk of marriage seemed like a frivolous irrelevance. With so many dying all around them, his one desire was that if God preserved him from the plague he would offer his life to train as an evangelist. Where did marriage fit in? How could he obey his father? Yet he dare not refuse. Both Christian teaching and Batak adat agreed that he should honour his father.

Ginjang was frowning at him as he stood there in silence. It was not, after all, an unusual suggestion, and Cleopas did not want to be thought a rebellious son. Respectfully he asked for time to think the matter over, and his father agreed.

"But I hope you'll come back shortly and tell me whose daughter you want, and then I can start the negotiations."

Cleopas went straight off to Pearaja, his head in a whirl. Nommensen was sitting in front of his house, recuperating. He listened carefully as Cleopas poured out the whole story — his father's demand, his own hopes and ambitions. Nommensen was not surprised. He had known this young man since he was fourteen, watched him grow and develop, and marked his longing to serve Christ. They prayed together about the future.

The next day Nommensen walked slowly down the hill to Saitnihuta.

"Ompu! Pendeta Nommensen!" beamed Raja Ginjang. "We thought you were sick! It's good to see you." He sent his daughter running to make tea, and ushered the missionary to a comfortable seat. "And how is Nyonya Nommensen? And all your children?"

"Oh, we're much better," said the missionary. "My family have all recovered, praise God. And I gather you've not suffered here so much as in some places."

"We've not done badly," agreed the raja. "There have been a few sick in the village, but only two deaths, and my own children have all recovered."

They agreed that the epidemic seemed to have run its course by now, and talked for a while of the many problems involved in caring for so many sick.

"Cleopas has been a great help," said Solomon. "He's been telling us about boiling our drinking water, and all that sort of thing. We're very clean here now, you know. Passing on what he's been taught at school."

"Yes," said Nommensen. "It's about Cleopas that I want to talk with you." He took a sip of the hot sweet tea. "I feel sure, Ompu Solomon, that the Lord is calling Cleopas to work in His vineyard. He's faithful, and gifted, and I hope that he will become a Bible teacher."

The raja smiled. "I hope so too, Pendeta."

"Good. Then we are both hoping for the same thing. We must think together about how we can best help him. These things don't just happen, you know, Ompu. He must work hard, and there will be obstacles to overcome."

"Obstacles? What sort of obstacles?"

"All sorts of obstacles." Nommensen waved his arm expansively. "The devil loves to make things difficult. There may be dangers, for instance. He's faced threats already, travelling to and from school. Or the problem of expenses for his training. There are many obstacles when we are seeking to do God's will. Obstacles can arise even from your own Batak traditions, your adat," he added.

Ginjang cleared his throat. "His expenses, I think, need not be a problem." He knew all about Nommensen's principle that the Batak students should pay their own way, and it accorded very well with his own notions of independence and self-respect. "But our adat now — how could that be an obstacle?"

"As you know, my dear Raja, Cleopas is now twenty years old. According to adat he should be getting married. But then, with a wife, it would be so much more difficult to study. He might fail. And think of all the responsibilities that go with marriage! It would be so much better if he didn't rush into it, at least until his studies are complete." Nommensen leaned forward to put a hand on the Batak's arm. "I'd like to ask you, Ompu Solomon, as his father, to advise Cleopas not to rush headlong into thoughts of marriage."

The raja nodded solemnly. "Ah yes, now I understand." He smiled. "Don't you worry, Pendeta Nommensen. You can leave that with me. I'll talk to Cleopas."

That very day Ginjang sent a servant to fetch his son. He told Cleopas all that Nommensen had said, and added that he hoped his son would work hard and be a good Bible teacher. It was quite something to have the benefits of all this new western teaching, and to be prized so highly by the German missionary.

"So you must forget about getting married for the time being," he added gruffly. "It's better to prepare yourself to serve God first."

"Yes, Father," agreed Cleopas. He thanked his father earnestly for all his help and encouragement, and assured him that he would never have cause to be ashamed of his son.

Cleopas sang for joy as he strolled back along the path to Pulopulo II.

PREPARATION 4

When the cholera epidemic had run its course, the missionaries in Silindung valley met together to discuss their future plans. It seemed clear that the travelling school could not reopen on its previous lines. Moving from one centre to another was unsettling and time-consuming and the informal nature of the school had made it difficult for the missionaries to give enough time to teaching.

"People come to see me at all times of the day and night," complained Mohri. "And if I happen to be teaching school, they think that doesn't matter — it's only a group of young lads!"

"Well, of course," said Nommensen mildly. "In Batak adat a visitor always takes precedence over anything else. We're very glad of that when we are the ones doing the visiting. And a grown man would naturally expect to be treated more respectfully than a lot of youngsters. This is a very hierarchical society, don't forget."

"But meanwhile the whole Batak Church is growing by leaps and bounds. Three thousand or more members already, and swarms of children wanting to come to the schools, and we've nowhere near enough people to teach them all."

"We're trying to do far too many things ourselves," said Nommensen. "Evangelism, medical work (especially in this last epidemic), teaching, preaching and administration. We should be training these young Batak Christians to share more in the ministry with us."

"We need someone who can give his whole time to training them. Not just the odd fragments of the day that aren't filled with other duties."

"In other words," said Johannsen, beating time on his paper with a well-used pen, "we need a proper seminary, with full-time teachers and full-time students."

They decided to build the new seminary at Pansur Napitu. Johannsen would be principal, with a newly arrived missionary as his assistant. Johannsen returned to Pansur Napitu to organize the building. Nommensen sent off a report to Barmen in Germany, and then invited each of the thirty travelling school students to come and see him.

Cleopas could hear the laughter as he climbed the steep path to Pearaja. A crowd of students had gathered under a tree outside the church. Joshua beckoned him across.

"We're starting school again," he said. "A real school, this time, in one place, and much more organized."

Cleopas was grinning as he walked over to Nommensen's office.

"Cleopas! Come in!" beamed Nommensen. "I've got some great news for you. Come and sit down here." He cleared a space among piles of papers — the first draft of a book of sermons in Batak. "We're going to have a new seminary, at Pansur Napitu, and I want you to continue your training there." He nodded encouragingly at Cleopas. "You've got a good record for hard work and enthusiasm so keep it up! I'm sure that Pendeta Johannsen will do his best to teach you well."

"Oh." Cleopas sat in silence, his face blank. "Is there not another seminary I could go to, somewhere else?" he asked at last.

"Another seminary?"

"My elder half brother, Ephraim, trained at Sipirok seminary before it closed down." Cleopas looked round the room for inspiration. "And my younger brother, Philemon... he can go to Pansur Napitu later perhaps. That's why I should like to go to a different school."

These did not seem very good reasons to Nommensen. He looked sharply at Cleopas, and began explaining again all the benefits of the new school. Eventually the real reason emerged.

"I don't get on with Mr Johannsen."

"Not get on with him! Why not?" Nommensen was astounded.

Cleopas gave a nervous cough. "Once, when we were in the travelling school," he explained. "Mr Johannsen was angry with me."

"Oh I see." Nommensen nodded. "Why was he angry?"

There was a long pause.

"Some of the others accused me of doing something that wasn't allowed. Mr Johannsen sent for me and questioned me about it." Cleopas stared at the ground for some moments before raising clear eyes to face Nommensen. "I didn't confess to it, because honestly, Pendeta, it wasn't me! I hadn't done what they said. I hadn't done anything wrong." Another pause. "But Mr Johannsen was very angry. He shouted."

Cleopas looked into the distance, remembering, and Nommensen watched him with thoughtful eyes.

"After that I always felt that he didn't trust me. There was something between us." He shrugged his shoulders. "I can't explain it. But I can't study at a seminary where Pendeta Johannsen is the principal."

What would they do now?

Nommensen sighed as he watched the young man walking off down the hill, his shoulders stiffly erect to hide his disappointment. Losing face was so devastating to these Bataks! But he could understand how Cleopas felt. As the son of a raja he was used to being honoured; and as head student, and at twenty a little older than the other students, he had been treated with respect in his own right. He would hate being spoken to like a child in front of the others. And shouted at! Losing one's temper was such a crime in this society where men so easily came to blows — maybe just because the consequences of losing control were so serious. Cleopas must have felt completely disgraced by the whole incident.

With another deep sigh the missionary took up his pen and began composing a letter to Johannsen.

A few days later Johannsen came to visit Cleopas at Pulopulo II. He told the young Batak about the preparations he had been making for the new seminary, and how much he hoped that Cleopas would take advantage of the opportunity to continue his education. He was confident, he said, that Cleopas had ability and would do well. But he did not mention the disagreement. Perhaps he was too embarrassed.

Cleopas felt dissatisfied. He thanked the missionary for coming, politely but coldly, and rejected the offer of a place at the seminary.

Johannsen did not easily give up. He went to see Cleopas's father, and Raja Solomon agreed to add his voice. But Cleopas held stubbornly to his decision.

Nommensen felt bitterly disappointed. Cleopas was usually so obedient, so faithful in every task he was given, and so ready to accept advice or rebuke. But in this one instance so obstinate! Yet Nommensen knew that Cleopas longed to teach. And after watching over the boy's development through the years, he longed to help him. Patient as always, the missionary began to look for another solution.

Some months later Nommensen asked Cleopas to go with him on a visit to Saitnihuta.

"Raja Solomon," he said, after all the formalities of greeting, and the enquiries as to the health and welfare of their various offspring, "I've brought Cleopas to see you, because I want to talk with you both about his education and his future ministry."

Ginjang looked up. He had long since despaired of this thick-headed son. "But is there a suitable school?"

"I'm sure you agree that it would be a shame, Ompu," said Nommensen, "if Cleopas were unable to continue his studies. We've both tried to persuade him to go to the seminary at Pansur Napitu, and he feels he can't do that. Well," he smiled across at Cleopas, "we can't insist. And you know that I would willingly have sent him to the new medical school at Sibolga instead," another smile. "Only he says he doesn't want to learn how to cut people up. So I'm sending someone else there, as I promised the doctor we'd send him a Batak student."

The raja frowned at his son. Yet another opportunity for education, and Cleopas had to turn it down!

"But I know that he is very eager to study," continued Nommensen. "He's always learning, always asking me questions about the things he doesn't understand. He wants to serve the Lord, and I know his prayer has always been that he might train as an evangelist."

Cleopas nodded his agreement.

"Well, I've been thinking and praying, and trying to work something out. And I think the best solution is to send him to a seminary in Java. So I've come to ask you, as his father, if you'll agree to send him to Java?"

Ginjang looked at the missionary. *How much this man loves my son!* he thought. He himself had never completely acknowledged the boy — even though he had made a home for him and had paid for his schooling.

"What do you think, son?" His voice trembled as he turned to Cleopas, but no one noticed. Cleopas was gazing at Nommensen, his face radiant.

"I would go to school anywhere if I can train as a Bible teacher," he declared. "Anywhere in the world except Pansur Napitu."

Nommensen laughed. "Well, in that case, Cleopas, we'll send you to West Java, to the seminary at Depok." He smiled at the raja. "Let's pray together, shall we, Ompu. We'll ask God's help and guidance in our plans."

Ginjang could hold back no longer. "My dear, dear Pendeta," he said earnestly, his words tumbling out in a great rush. "I want to thank you from the bottom of my heart for coming here to our country. If you hadn't come and taught us, I should never have cared at all for my son here, or his brother and sister. Or for their mother either. In fact" — he paused — "I might even have killed him one day!" A great shudder passed through the raja's body. "I might have killed my own son," he whispered. "— all because a datu told me that if he lived he would overthrow my kingdom and destroy our traditions."

There was a long silence. The raja clearly had more on his mind, and Nommensen waited patiently till he was ready to unburden himself.

Ginjang took a great gulp of air. He was not at all accustomed to sharing his feelings or to letting go of his dignity.

"When I became a Christian," he said eventually, "you prompted me to meet with my first wife and her children again. I built a new village for them. But all the time, until now, I have had a great big blockage which stopped me from loving them — especially from loving this son." He stared at the ground. "But when I see how much care and trouble *you've* taken over him and hear you speak about all *your* hopes for him ... He's not *your* son. You aren't even a Lumbantobing ... You're not a Batak even!"

Nommensen smiled.

"I feel ashamed. I've never cared much what happened to that family. For a long time now this son has tried to get near me, but I wouldn't have it. I always got angry and pushed him away." He looked at Cleopas and sighed. "But he never looked for revenge. He tried only to please me. And all the time in my heart, I just can't forget the datu's curse."

Solomon turned to Nommensen, his face drained.

"I want you to pray for me, that God will forgive me and give me strength. I promise that in future I'll do all that our adat requires for Cleopas, and for his brother Moses and his sister Hannah, and for their mother my first wife, Boru Hutabarat."

Nommensen's eyes were moist as he took the raja's hands in

his own strong grip. "Thank you," he said. "It's very good that you could share this so openly and honestly."

Very gently he prayed for the father and son, praising God for Solomon's confession and asking Him to strengthen the raja's faith; claiming the victory, in Jesus' name, over any evil influence still lingering from the augury.

Cleopas took the hand his father offered. He tried to say something, words of reassurance or forgiveness, but his throat was choked with tears and no words came. They embraced in silence. As they left, Nommensen reminded the raja that he must never go back on a promise made before God.

"Don't neglect your responsibilities to your first wife. And don't make any distinction between her children and those of your present wife, Boru Manik."

It was almost a year before the preparations were completed. The seminary at Depok accepted applications for a group of seven young men from Silindung valley to train as Bible teachers. On January 11, 1880 they gathered at Pearaja for a farewell service: Cleopas, Christian, Abel, Peter, Joshua, Benjamin and Luke.

Nommensen reminded them in his sermon that they must pray constantly and walk faithfully in the way of Jesus, who would keep them safe from all harm. After the service, and a great feast of pork and buffalo with many speeches, the missionary gave Cleopas letters of introduction to the harbour official at Sibolga and to the principal of the seminary.

The friends set off together on their two day trek to the coast. Each carried a bundle on his shoulder and some money in his pocket.

Just like all the times we set off on the travelling school circuit, thought Cleopas, as he turned to wave a last goodbye. But his thumping heart told him otherwise. They had never before been out of the Silindung valley. None of them had ever seen the sea.

Sibolga was bewildering in its bustle and busyness. After many times asking the way on the crowded streets, they found the harbour office and presented their letter to the man on duty. He quickly arranged for some sailors to row them out to a ship which was standing at anchor in the bay.

As the ship set sail for South Sumatra, Cleopas and his friends looked back with longing at the dark green mountains rising up behind the port of Sibolga. Their ship was sturdy but small, twenty to forty tons. The young Bataks felt seasick even before they were out of the bay, and by the time they docked at Bengkulu they were all so ill that they scarcely knew what was happening. A two-day break while cargo was unloaded and loaded gave them some relief. The friends crawled ashore and strolled round the harbour, a row of drab buildings guarded by Dutch soldiers.

Once more the ship set sail. At first they coped better with the constant rise and fall of the waves. Then towards afternoon it began to rain — lightly at first, but with increasing force the further they went. The pale grey sky deepened to an ominous purple, and the rain thudded down relentlessly on the heaving sea. The little boat was tossed about like a coconut shell, a plaything of the Indian Ocean. The passengers clung terrified to the lurching sides. Never in their wildest nightmares had the seven young Bataks imagined such horror. Desperately they prayed for safety. And still the rain hurtled down.

Crew and passengers worked together, struggling to move about in the wildly rocking boat, bailing out water. But however fast they bailed, it seemed they could never keep pace with the pouring rain and the angry seawater lashing over the side.

And then even to stand was too much. They sank down exhausted in a sheltered corner, soaked to the skin and numb with cold. Cleopas shivered. A sudden flare lit up the ocean, showing his friends' faces as frightened as his own. They listened to the thunder's growl.

I'm the oldest, thought Cleopas, *and I should be the leader.* He took a deep breath.

"My friends," he shouted, "I'm quite sure the Lord won't abandon us!" His voice drifted away on the wind, and he strained harder to make himself heard. "It's the Lord who is sending us to Java ... We're only going there so we can serve him." His chest heaved as he forced the air through his lungs with rasping breaths. "If it's His will for us to go there — and I'm sure it is — then He won't forget to take care of us!"

"No... of course He won't," gasped Joshua.

They smiled at each other. "The same Jesus who made the sea calm at Galilee," said Cleopas, his faith stronger suddenly with the memory.

The others nodded, still afraid, but remembering again who it was they believed in.

"Let's pray together."

Some time later the storm lessened its force. The rain stopped, and the waves gradually calmed down. The sharp tang of fear was sweetened with relief. In their sheltered corner the Batak Christians remembered to thank God for His protection, as Nommensen had taught them. Cleopas felt as if he had been through a tremendous battering; not just in the thunderstorm, but in his whole being. He felt that he had emerged with an unshakeable conviction of God's love.

Wearily they began to sort through their sodden baggage.

"Oh no! My money's gone!" Peter was panic-stricken. Hurriedly he ran his fingers through his bundle, spilling out the contents onto the deck. No money. The others did the same. Their money was intact, only Peter's, about twenty silver dollars in all, was missing. He looked round wildly. Whatever could he do, so far from home, with no money?

They reported the loss to the captain, who shook his head.

"There are thirty passengers on this ship, including yourselves," he said. "It would be quite impossible to search them all. I'm afraid there's nothing I can do."

"Well!" Peter was annoyed. "What shall I do then?"

The friends talked it over and agreed that each would give Peter something to make good his loss. And at the same time they would write to Silindung to ask Nommensen for help.

On January 21 the ship landed at the port of Pasar Ikan. To their great relief, someone from the seminary was waiting to meet the new students and take them to Depok, about twenty kilometres away.

Clutching their crumpled bundles and looking round in some awe at the smartly dressed Javanese students, the Bataks trooped into the principal's office to be introduced. He was a tall, mild-looking man, with shrewd eyes and a direct way of talking which soon made them feel at home. He showed them the hostel behind his house where they would be living and explained to them, in careful Malay, the rules and regulations of the seminary.

"You are a whole semester late," he added. "It's not your fault, so don't worry. I'm sure if you work hard, you'll be able to catch up with the others."

They lined up to sign the register. Cleopas felt a thrill of pride as he wrote his name with a flourish: Cleopas Lumbantobing, from Saitnihuta, Silindung: Seminary Student.

WATER ... OF LIFE? 5

The three-year course at Depok was followed by six months' practical experience when the young men worked in pairs in congregations and mission posts in West Java.

One of the Bataks, Peter, had been forced to drop out part way through the course, after a severe attack of smallpox kept him in bed for four months. The remaining six, newly qualified as Bible teachers, returned to Silindung in September 1883.

The valley looked sleek and prosperous, Cleopas thought, and the children who ran to greet them seemed plumper and friendlier. Or was it simply that this was home and there was no place in the world like it?

"Well, we don't have quite so many wars now," explained Peter, who had come halfway down to Sibolga to meet the new graduates and escort them back up the mountains. "And we have far more Christians than before. There was a big Church Conference at Pearaja two years ago, and 3,500 people came. Just imagine!"

"Almost the whole valley!" murmured Cleopas.

"There've been lots of changes. You'll see. We farm the land differently, for one thing. Everyone goes out together to the paddyfields, and we plant together and cut the paddy together. We don't just work our own land our own way like we used to, and because we're doing it together, we seem to get more rice."

"And so you get richer," said Joshua, looking round appreciatively.

They were entering Tarutung, the capital for the Dutch colonial administration in Silindung valley. It was now a large town with smart government offices and a police station. Nommensen's home at Pearaja, up the hill, was its ecclesiastical suburb. Cleopas gasped as he saw the magnificent new buildings — a church, church office, rectory and school.

A huge crowd of people was waiting in front of the church to welcome them, and a fanfare of trumpets boomed out in greeting. The graduates gazed in amazement at the proud uniforms and shiny instruments of the Batak Protestant Christian Church Brass Band.

"Lots of changes," repeated Peter, grinning proudly.

Nommensen himself had been away while the students were in Java, taking his first furlough after eighteen years in Sumatra. He spent a busy year visiting congregations in Germany, telling them all that God was doing among the Batak people, thanking them for their prayers and support, and urging more Christians to join them in the work.

Returning to Sumatra, Nommensen was appointed by the Rhenish Mission Society to the new position of "Ephorus" ("overseer" or bishop) of the Batak Church. The church office at Pearaja became the administrative centre of the Church, while Nommensen himself pursued a roving ministry. Later he settled at Sigumpar, on the shore of Lake Toba.

As Nommensen's wife had been lame since her illness in 1872, she felt increasingly unable to cope with the Batak mountains. Their children were needing a German education: the eldest was already thirteen. So Nommensen had returned alone to Sumatra, leaving his wife and four children in Germany. It was a costly decision. He never saw his wife again. She died five and a half years later, in March 1887.

The bishop was thrilled to see the new graduates. He called a meeting straight away to assign them to their workplaces. Some would be assistants to the missionaries in various districts of Batakland, others would teach in the schools or work as evangelists and Bible teachers in the churches.

Cleopas was appointed in sole charge of the congregation at Simorangkir, just south of Tarutung, as the German missionary there was involved in wider church responsibilities.

"There's a bit of a problem at Simorangkir just now," Nommensen warned Cleopas. "So tread warily."

"A problem?"

"They've been Christians at Simorangkir for a long time, as you know," said Nommensen. "Mr Johannsen visited them first of all, and then about ten years ago the chief raja gave us land for a church. There must have been seventy people baptized at that time."

"And now?"

"There's a man living there now called Sibasir, a religious teacher. Calls himself a Muslim, but I'm not so sure."

Cleopas was surprised. Islam had a strong base already in the southern part of Batakland, spreading inward from the fiercely Muslim Minangkabau area on the west coast of Sumatra. But the Silindung valley had so far been a Christian preserve.

"Sibasir has been there about four years now," continued the bishop. "He arrived just before you went off to Java."

"Oh yes! I remember now. I've met him. We had heated words, I remember."

"Well, we are Christians," said Nommensen with his gentle smile. "We preach the Gospel of Jesus Christ, who alone has the power to save us from our sins and to give eternal life. But we don't use force to persuade people. So take a firm stand on what you believe, and then you must leave people the freedom to make up their own minds."

Cleopas nodded.

"And remember to pray for them."

It seemed that Sibasir had quite a following in Simorangkir. He had prophesied a golden age, soon to come, when the whole Silindung valley would be converted to Islam with the coming of a great religious leader, Tuan (Lord) Syech. In preparation for this glorious time, he urged his disciples to build a fine house for Tuan Syech. And when the leader failed to appear, he told them that he himself had been appointed to live there in the meantime. He also explained at some length that the villagers must pay him a special tax — a freewill offering from the best of their crops at the end of the fasting month.

Not long after Cleopas moved to Simorangkir he heard that Sibasir had in his possession some miraculous spring water, with power to give life to the dead and restore what had decayed. He would give the water freely to all who promised to follow his teaching and learned to recite the Muslim creed. People were flocking to Simorangkir from miles around, tumbling over themselves in their eagerness to learn the Muslim creed and obtain the water.

"It's pure superstition," grumbled Cleopas. "Nothing to do with Islam really. It's like something out of our old Batak religion — spirit worship or something. *Pengabang-abang pengubang-ubang,* he calls it."

"Well, yes, that does sound more like Batak than Arabic," agreed Nommensen. "What do the words mean, do you think?"

"Mmm. Well." Cleopas considered. They were sitting in the church office in Pearaja, whither he had fled in despair for some fatherly comfort and advice. "It's a play on words really. It could mean one of those big birds, hovering on the wing, ..."

"Sparrow hawk, you mean?"

"That's right. Hovering on the wing, high up in a clear blue sky — just before it swoops down to pounce on a poor little rat in the rice stubble." He laughed. "Or it could mean madness hovering about your head, just about to drive you out of your mind."

"Oh really! Got a sense of humour, then, this Sibasir."

"Maybe he believes it himself. Everyone else seems to. But I don't think so. I think he's tricking them all." Cleopas frowned. "And I don't know what to do about it."

"Do nothing," said Nommensen. "Not yet. We'll pray about it, and keep calm, and wait. And pray some more." He smiled. "The Lord will sort it all out."

Soon after this a wealthy man in the village died. His relatives rushed immediately to Sibasir's house, to beg him for some magic water.

"Can you recite the Muslim creed?" he asked.

"We can't, we've had no opportunity to learn it," said the widow. "But we will learn it, willingly. We'll follow your teaching, if only you'll let us have some special water."

"You must give me your firm promise, then," Sibasir said sternly, "that you will come here every day until you've learned to recite the creed." He looked round the family group. "All of you."

Readily they agreed to his conditions; they would have agreed to anything he demanded, for the hope of bringing the dead to life.

In cautious haste they carried the water back to the house. With hands and cloths they washed the dead man's body with the precious water, leaving it to dry naturally on his skin. They were afraid to pat or rub it in case they rubbed away its potency. Then they dressed him in his finest clothes, and covered him up to his chin with the special black blanket which was used to honour the dead. They sat down in silence and waited; the widow by her husband's head, and the children grouped around in order of age and sex.

All this time they were expecting him at any moment to sit up, to smile, to speak to them. They waited in the thickening darkness, but the corpse remained a corpse. Night passed, and morning came, and the man lay still. And as they waited, the scent of decay was growing stronger, until a decision had to be taken. It was time for burial.

Another family, and then another, had the same experience. They learned the creed, they took the water, they were sure that their dead would rise, but nothing happened. Some waited hours, some days, until the smell of rotting flesh was too strong and it was unmistakeably clear that the corpse would never live again.

A crowd of villagers went to Sibasir's house to demand an explanation.

"You didn't believe enough," said the religious teacher. He spoke slowly and deliberately, to make sure they all understood. "Your faith was too weak. The power of my holy water depends entirely on your faith in it. The water will restore the dead if you believe in it. You are doubting still. So of course it failed." He smiled round at his hearers. "You need more teaching. You need to come to me more often, to study, so that you can recite the creed more perfectly."

Some accepted this explanation, but many were dismayed. They had been totally convinced that the miraculous water had power to bring life to the dead. How could their faith have been too weak? No one could have believed more than they did. Gradually doubts arose about Sibasir's teaching.

Cleopas had been following these events closely, and he was quick to seize his opportunity. He visited the local rajas one by one, beginning with the man who ten years before had first given land to build the church and school in Simorangkir. He told them that their people were the victims of a fraud and that Sibasir's water could not possibly bring dead people back to life.

"There *is* a life-giving water which is far more wonderful than that," said Cleopas. The Lord Jesus has promised to give the living water of eternal life to everyone who believes in Him. And even though we die, if we believe in Jesus we shall live together with Him in Heaven. But that is completely different from a magic water, like this man offers, to revive rotting corpses."

He reminded the rajas of their responsibility as leaders of society to show their rejection of Sibasir's teaching. And when he felt they had accepted his arguments, he went to the marketplace and into the fields and talked with the people he met there.

At first no one listened. They said Cleopas was spying for the

Dutch, that he, not Sibasir, was the one who wanted to trick them.

But time went by and the miraculous water never succeeded in bringing anyone back to life, and the long-awaited Tuan Syech failed to appear. So the tide of opinion began to change. Maybe, after all, Sibasir was just a trickster who wanted to live in a fine house and was greedy for a share in their farming profits. Yes, that's what he was — a greedy trickster who wanted to grow fat on the fruits of *their* hard work! The whole village seethed with indignation.

Early in the new year the raja sent his men to order Sibasir to leave Simorangkir. He refused.

"I have come here to live and work because Allah the Almighty sent me here," he proclaimed. "Neither you nor anyone else has the right to send me away."

The men stalked off in a rage to report to the raja.

Cleopas was just coming out of his house as the raja swept down the track towards Sibasir's house, with a pack of angry Bataks baying at his heels.

"What is it? Where are you going?" He grabbed someone's arm as the crowd swept by. "What's happened?"

"You were right, Teacher," said the boy. "That Sibasir's an imposter! The raja's ordered him to leave, but he won't go! So we're off to throw him out!"

"Oh, but..."

"Come on and we'll get him!"

Sibasir was not at home, his servants told them, he was on the river bank, praying. Off they went to the river.

Cleopas followed them at a distance. He heartily disliked and distrusted this man Sibasir, who exploited people's grief with his false teaching. But the crowd looked blood-hungry, and Cleopas felt responsible.

Sibasir was standing with his arms in the air, chanting dolefully. He knelt down and bowed his head to the ground with expansive, sweeping gestures, unlike anything the raja had seen before.

"Get up!" shouted the raja. "Up with you! You must leave this village immediately!"

Sibasir ignored them. With a set face and closed eyes he continued the ritual of worship.

The Bataks did not understand this form of praying. Furiously the whole crowd surged forward. A sturdy young soldier caught hold of Sibasir by the scruff of his neck and was all set to give him a thrashing when Cleopas came rushing up.

"Don't! Don't! Stop! Wait!" He stood there panting, while the soldier kept tight hold of his prisoner.

"Don't spill this man's blood!" gasped Cleopas. "If he's done wrong, then the raja should try him properly and pass judgment. Or the government courts."

"Hmm." The soldier raised his hand to strike.

"Don't let anyone accuse you of being cowards — many of you to attack one weak and foolish little man!"

Cowards? The soldier paused a moment, then turned suddenly and with a shout threw Sibasir out into the river.

"Now go!"

The river was shallow and wide. Sibasir hurriedly picked himself up and stumbled across to the opposite bank while his accusers yelled abuse after him. He clambered onto the bank, hoisted up his sarung, and ran off.

It was nearing midday when a Dutch policeman arrived in Simorangkir, looking for Cleopas.

"Good day, officer, can I help you?" asked the Bible teacher.

"You must come back with me straight away to the police station in Tarutung."

Cleopas stared at him. "Yes, of course, if you like. But why?"

"A Mr Sibasir has accused you of assaulting him and causing grievous bodily harm."

"Sibasir? Assaulting him? Accused *me*?"

Like wildfire the news spread round the village that Cleopas had been arrested on charges brought by Sibasir. A huge escort (including the man who had thrown Sibasir into the river) turned out to accompany them to the police station.

"You have all of you broken the law," said the officer in charge. "Why did you attack Sibasir? He claims you've injured him."

"That's not true!" yelled a young Batak, leaning so far over the desk that the officer hurriedly moved his chair back.

"Nobody touched Sibasir!"

"He's making it all up! We never hit him!"

"Let's see him then!" demanded the warrior. "Bring him out and let's see the proof, if he says the teacher here struck him!"

The officer nodded. A side door was opened and Sabosir was led out.

"Is this the man who struck you?" asked the officer, pointing to Cleopas.

Sibasir nodded.

"Open your shirt, then, and let's see your bruises."

Sibasir stood still.

"Open your shirt," ordered the officer.

Reluctantly he took off his shirt. There was no sign of injury.

"Show us, then!" said the officer angrily. "Where were you beaten? Show us the marks!"

Sibasir stood in silence, his head lowered.

"Oh, take him away!" The officer waved his hand impatiently. "You can lock him up on a charge of slander!"

The officer turned to Cleopas as Sibasir was led out. "What was all that about then? What's your version of what happened?"

Cleopas explained how Sibasir had been deceiving the people, and that when they realized this the villagers had been so angry that they had ordered him out of town. When he refused to leave, they had driven him out. But they had not actually beaten him.

"I very nearly did," admitted the young soldier. "I would have given him a beating, but it was the Bible teacher here who stopped me. So I threw him into the river instead."

"Oh, I see." The officer stroked his moustache to hide a smile, and thanked them all for their explanation. "You may go now."

It took a long time for the gospel to take root in Simorangkir. People were wary, perhaps, after being deceived by one teacher of religion. Though they chatted with Cleopas in a friendly way, few at first would join his catechism class.

Patiently Cleopas continued his visits in the area, each day a different village, building up relationships, encouraging those who showed interest. Gradually over the months he gathered together a group who wanted to learn — not so much the Christian faith, but the reading, writing and arithmetic which Cleopas also offered them. Whatever their motives, the teacher rejoiced as he struggled with them over words and sentences. One day, he hoped, they would be reading the Bible for themselves, and that would surely draw them into God's kingdom.

LIKE LAMBS AMONG WOLVES 6

One day Raja Tinggi came to visit Raja Ginjang.

"Ompu Solomon," began Tinggi, after they had exhausted the preliminary enquiries about the health of their children and the state of their crops, "I want you to do something for me. You helped me before, I remember, when I had a problem with the Dutch Company. And now I hope you will speak to Bishop Nommensen for me. You know him well, I'm sure, and I want you to be my middleman."

"Yes, of course," said Ginjang. "But what's your problem?"

"Oh — no problem," said Tinggi with an airy wave of the hand. "I want you to ask him to send us your son Cleopas to live in my village and to teach us the Christian religion."

"Oh, you do!" Ginjang gave him a searching look. "Why must it be Cleopas?"

Tinggi shrugged. "He's the ideal person. He's a Batak, so he's not limited by the Company's prohibitions as the missionaries are. And even more important, because he's a Batak he won't be treated as an enemy by Sisingamangaraja."

"Yes, that's true." Ginjang nodded thoughtfully.

The Dutch East India Company did not usually allow westerners to settle in areas not yet under Company control. And the Lake Toba region to the north of Silindung was dominated by the infamous Sisingamangaraja, who hated Christians and white imperialists with equal fervour.

Sisingamangaraja was one of a line of Batak chieftains who were honoured and respected for their godlike powers. "Sisingamangaraja is a visible god whose spirit we can know," went the saying, and most Bataks stood in awe of this half-mythical leader. He became a central symbol of resistance to growing Dutch influence in Sumatra, and would be remembered later as a pioneer of the Independence Movement.

When Nommensen had baptized his first converts at Huta Dame, in 1865, it seems that the spirits of the ancestors fled in a rage to Lake Toba (to the terror of the Bataks living there) complaining volubly to Sisingamangaraja XI. White men had come to Silindung, they told him, who would entice the Batak people away from the religion of their ancestors into new and strange beliefs.

Sisingamangaraja had immediately ordered the rajas of Silindung to muster an army. They would march together to attack and destroy the missionary settlement at Huta Dame. But a quarrel broke out between the great leader and Raja Pontas, already half-converted to Christianity at that stage. Sisingamangaraja was forced to withdraw.

Twelve years later his son, Sisingamangaraja XII, swept down with an army of Acehnese, the fierce Muslim tribe from the northern tip of Sumatra. They threatened to drive out or murder all the whites, and all Bataks who had forsaken ancestor worship. But Dutch troops arrived with reinforcements from Sibolga and drove back Sisingamangaraja's army. The Dutch pressed on in revenge to subdue the whole area as far as Lake Toba, burning down villages as they went.

The horrified Nommensen had worked tirelessly for peace. He implored the Dutch commander to slow down, sought out the Batak rajas who had fled for safety, and helped to negotiate a peace agreement. A small garrison of Dutch soldiers was established at Laguboti, by Lake Toba, and another at Sipoholon in Silindung valley, with a Dutch district officer in residence at Tarutung. Thus the colonial government strengthened its control in North Sumatra.

During the resulting period of peace, Toba Bataks visited

Silindung and were struck by the signs of material progress. Rajas and even datus bought copies of the Batak New Testament translated by Nommensen. Some asked for missionaries to be sent to their villages on the southern shore of Lake Toba, and to open schools there.

However, many felt the westerners were still too closely associated with colonial power. In 1883 Sisingamangaraja launched a final desperate attack on the Dutch Company, unleashing a wave of violence throughout the whole Toba and Silindung region. Missionaries' homes were burnt down and the church at Sipoholon was destroyed, along with the army barracks. The Dutch retaliated by attacking Sisingamangaraja's headquarters at Bakara.

And now Raja Tinggi wanted Cleopas to teach the Christian Gospel by Lake Toba! Ginjang chewed on his lip as he gazed at his friend.

"We have a missionary now in Laguboti," continued Raja Tinggi. "Pendeta Bonn from Germany. Very friendly. He used to come round every market day, selling his books and telling us stories about Jesus. But he lived a long way off in those days — almost at Sisingamangaraja's village. And then when we had all that uproar last year, his house was burnt down."

"Burnt down?"

"He wasn't there, of course. Plenty of warning was given and his wife and children got out right away." The raja shook his head. "It was hard going for Pendeta Bonn though. He was there in the thick of it. The bishop wanted to go and fetch him, but no one would accompany him. Frightened, the lot of them! And who wouldn't be frightened of Sisingamangaraja!"

"Who indeed!" Ginjang murmured his agreement.

"But he was all right. That's what amazes me about this god Jesus they're telling us about!" Tinggi looked at Ginjang. "Very powerful! Don't you think so?"

Ginjang nodded.

"I sometimes wonder if his power is even greater than that of the ancestors." Tinggi shook his head. "He saved the missionary, anyway. Not by magic though," he added. "The old raja from that little island just off shore came and rescued him in the middle of the night, and brought him round by boat. But Mr Bonn says it was his god who was looking after him."

"Yes. I'm sure it was."

"Ye-es." The raja shook his head again. "I don't understand it all yet, but I'm sure it's good, and it's going to help my people. It's going to bring progress!" he slapped his thigh with a decisive palm. "So we've built a house and a school for the missionary, and he's promised to make Laguboti a centre for teaching us about the Christian faith."

"And where does my son Cleopas fit into all this?"

"Ah, well, you see," Ompu Tinggi leant forward to trace a map on the ground with his finger. "This is my village, Lumban Bagasan Toba, just here. There's a big bay here, where the foot of the lake sticks out, and my village is right across the bay from Laguboti. It's outside Dutch territory. You couldn't have a missionary living in my village. But you could have a Batak Bible teacher."

"So you could," said Ginjang. "Just leave it to me, Ompu. I'll speak to Bishop Nommensen about it."

Nommensen was delighted to hear of an opening for further outreach in the "forbidden territories." But Raja Ginjang had one condition to make.

"Cleopas is almost thirty years old now — well past the age of settling down and giving me some grandsons. Before you move him to Lake Toba, I hope you will tell him he must first get married."

"And so you see, Cleopas," explained the bishop a few days later. "This is a tremendous opportunity to share the gospel in a region quite outside the influence of the Dutch Government. It won't be easy, though. Here in Silindung we've got used to a Christian lifestyle. There the people will be strangers to you, and you'll be up against the datus and the evil spirits. You'll face certain opposition. It's a spiritual battle you'll be going into." He paused. "But God will go with you. Are you willing?"

"Yes, Ompu."

"Good." Nommensen beamed at him. "But there's something we need to sort out first. Your father insists that this time you get married before you go."

Cleopas grinned.

"And he's quite right too. You need someone to be a friend and companion. It'll be lonely at first in Toba. A good wife will keep you steadfast in the hard work ahead of you." He straightened the papers on his desk. "And I have to tell you, Cleopas, that Raja Solomon has already picked out a prospective bride for you. Unless you have someone particular in mind?" He looked a question, but the young man's face was impassive. "So I suggest you go and see your father straight away and talk it over with him."

On February 10, 1885, Cleopas Lumbantobing and Petronella Boru Pohan-Simanjuntak were married by Bishop Nommensen. Eight days later the bishop gave the newly-weds his blessing, commissioning them to minister the gospel to the Toba Bataks.

It took three days to walk the sixty kilometres to Laguboti, stopping overnight at villages they passed on the way. At Bonn's house they rested for a few days, and the missionary introduced them to the new Christian groups he had started in the district with the help of his Batak assistant, a graduate from the seminary at Pansur Napitu. Cleopas too would be responsible to Bonn, but he would be working very much on his own. "He can stand on his own feet," Nommensen assured Bonn in his letter of introduction.

Bonn hoped it was true. Riots or warfare between villages were frequent in those areas not yet under Company control, where there was no authority strong enough to guarantee peace.

"The Lord will go with you, I'm sure," Bonn told the young couple as he prayed with them before sending them on the last stage of their journey. "And you have a powerful sponsor in Ompu Tinggi."

The raja was waiting to greet them at Lumban Bagasan Toba, where a fine new house had been built for them and pigs slaughtered for a welcoming feast. Ompu Tinggi ceremonially introduced Cleopas to his people as the son of his very good friend Ompu Ginjang of Silindung. He related the long list of benefits he expected his people to gain from the promised education and from the new Christian religion. They must respect Teacher Cleopas, he said, as they would respect the raja's own sons. He glared round at this point, in a silent reminder of what might result if this warning passed unheeded.

"Thank you for your welcome, Ompu Tinggi," said Cleopas in his reply. "I'm sure that you will gain much from the Christian teaching, and I very much hope that we will be able to share with you what we have learned about the God of Love."

Ompu Tinggi's protection did much to ease the way for the young couple in their early days in Lumbun Bagasan Toba. But it soon became clear that the Toba Bataks resented the new arrivals. Petronella met with cold looks when she went to the market or to fetch water from the lake; and Cleopas's friendly smile was answered with scowls or muttered threats. He wore trousers and shirt in the Dutch style. This was second nature to him after his years as a student and not at all out of place in progressive Silindung. But here all the men still wore sarungs. The smart clothes marked Cleopas out as a possible Dutch agent and increased the Bataks' antagonism.

Night after night Cleopas and Petronella were startled out of their sleep by rifle shots, or stones being thrown at the house. Sometimes in the early morning they would find little bundles of herbs or twigs arranged in strange patterns under the steps of the house — evil tokens to frighten them, potent with harmful intent.

Cleopas swept them away or burnt them.

"Greater is He that is in us than he that is in the world," he would proclaim, with a vigorous sweep of the broom.

But Petronella had not had the benefits of four years of theological training. Her faith had grown, like that of many Batak Christian girls, in a much more hit-and-miss environment. The powers of the datu were still very real to her. Rising before dawn to fetch the water and to pound the rice, as a good Batak wife should, became a torture. How could she be the first to climb down the steps, when unknown evil powers might lurk there to attack?

Cleopas prayed and smiled and continued to visit his neighbours however often he was repulsed, and to share the gospel whenever he could. Sometimes he would tramp for miles through the countryside, calling at distant villages, or stopping to chat with people working in the fields.

As for Petronella, she felt as if she were going out of her mind. A housewife for the first time in her life, she had no one to turn to — no mother-in-law near to guide her, no younger sister to help with the fetching and carrying, no friends to gossip or joke with. Only a solid wall of hate. Paralysed with fear, she would barricade herself into the house whenever Cleopas went out, and cry and cry.

One morning Cleopas awoke to see his wife standing by the fireplace, staring down in horror at a small object on the floor. Coming closer, he saw that it was a sweet potato, roughly hollowed out and filled with an evil-smelling paste.

"Never mind," he said. "It's just nonsense." He bent down to pick up the potato and tossed it carelessly on to the pile of firewood. "It can't harm us. It's all nonsense."

Petronella was shaking violently, and he put his arm round her shoulder to calm her.

"It's all right," he murmured. "Never mind."

"Even ... in ... the ... house!" She drew in breath between each word, trying to control the sobs which racked her tense body. "They even ... come ... into the house ... when we're sleeping ... and leave ... That Thing!"

"Yes, they did." He held her tightly, willing her to calm down. "But they didn't harm us, did they? Because God was watching over us to protect us."

"God!" She wrenched free of his grasp and swung round, accusing. "Why can't you tell *Ompu Tinggi* what they're doing to us?" It was an old cry. They had had this out many times before. "Ompu Tinggi will protect us! He'd be furious if he knew what was happening! They would never dare to harm us if Ompu Tinggi came and put a stop to it!"

"But listen, Love — just think a bit. If we complain about all these people to Ompu Tinggi — oh yes, he'll be angry with them. He'll rage through here and they won't know what's hit them! He'll stop it for now." Cleopas smiled gently. "But don't you see that people will only hate us more than ever? We'll never get to share the gospel with them."

"I can't take it." Petronella sank to her knees, her head in her hands. "I can't take it any more. How much longer do we have to go on living in a place where everybody hates us?"

Cleopas watched her helplessly. He had no idea how to cope with the situation.

"All the time, they're trying to get rid of us. They're just going on and on, trying to get rid of us."

Slowly he sat down on the floor beside her.

"What can we do?" She sat back on her heels and looked across at him, her eyes red raw.

Cleopas sat in silence for a moment. "Remember what the bishop said," he murmured. "The one who sends us, even to Toba, is not a man. Not the bishop, nor the people in the church office. It's God Almighty and the Lord Jesus Christ. It's like He sent out His disciples, like He sent out the seventy, to live as lambs among wolves."

Petronella looked at him without speaking.

"That's what I hold on to when it seems too hard," he said more firmly. Remember that verse the bishop read us, from Isaiah Chapter 41? 'Do not fear, for I am with you.'"

There was a long pause.

"I remember."

"Wait. I'll get my Bible and we'll read it again together."

Cleopas dashed across the room to fetch the Bible from its place on the chest. When he came back, his wife was sitting crosslegged, wiping her eyes on her shawl. He sat down beside her and opened the book on his knee.

"Here's the place. Let's read it together, mmm?"

He smiled tentatively, and she nodded. Solemnly they read the words out loud.

"So do not fear for I am with you;
do not be dismayed, for I am your God.
I will strengthen you and help you.
I will uphold you with my righteous right hand."

Cleopas laid the Bible carefully on the floor beside him. "I do believe that the Lord has brought us to this village." He paused. "Do you believe that, Petronella?"

"Yes." The whisper was so faint that he barely caught it. He looked at her bent head and did not like to ask again.

"So I'm convinced that He will look after us. I think we should make a firm promise now to be patient, and to hold on to God's promise in this verse." He paused again. "Do you agree?"

In trepidation he waited for her answer. He could not think what they would do if she said no.

But she raised her eyes to his, and her lips mouthed a very costly but determined "Yes."

They smiled at each other. Cleopas gave a deep sigh.

"Let's pray together," he said. "Let's pray together for our enemies."

7 THE PENDETA

The terrorism continued. The Toba Bataks spied continually on Cleopas and his wife, astonished that they remained healthy and showed no animosity towards their tormentors. Petronella still had to steel herself to go out. But she tried to smile at her neighbours, and slowly, very slowly, they became less brusque. Cleopas chatted with people whenever he could, and instead of rejecting his visits, some of the men even began to seek him out occasionally. Often Petronella would go with Cleopas on his visits. Talking over their problems and fears and praying together about them helped her to cope with the loneliness. They drew closer as a couple, much closer than was usual among Bataks at that time.

Not all the hatred was directed against the Lumbantobings. Fights were constantly breaking out among the Toba Bataks themselves, often over seemingly trivial causes. Long-lasting family feuds and jealousies were common.

Like Nommensen in earlier days, Cleopas was always on hand with his first aid box. As he bound up their wounds, he would tell the men about Jesus, the bringer of peace. Some of the older children became adept at judging when an ugly scene had reached the point at which they must run to fetch the teacher. Cleopas as a middleman could end the fight without either side losing face. But the good news he had come to share with them seemed to make little impact.

One afternoon, as Cleopas and his wife rested in their house they heard a sudden burst of rapid gunfire, followed by shouts.

Cleopas rushed to the narrow slit in the boards that did duty as a window.

"An attack!"

Squabbles over an unpaid gambling debt had led to war being declared between Lumban Bagasan Toba and another village. Now Ompu Tinggi's army had been pressed right back, and forced to take refuge in the village. Enemy forces were climbing the mud-brick walls and thrusting their way in through the prickly bamboo thicket.

Women and children screamed with terror as they scattered in all directions, looking for hiding places. A long spear with a trailing red cloth streamer hurtled through the air, and then a hailstorm of stone missiles from the enemy catapults thudded down on the walls and roofs of houses. The attackers gave blood-curdling yells as they leaped into combat with the few guards defending the walls.

Cleopas and Petronella looked at each other in alarm. With clasped hands they prayed quietly together, reminding themselves and the Lord of His promise of protection, and committing their own welfare, and that of the village, into His strong keeping.

"Stay here!" said Cleopas. "Don't on any account go out. Just pray!"

"Be careful!"

"Don't worry."

Cleopas gave his wife's shoulder a gentle squeeze then slithered hastily down the steps and out into the square. He was stopped in his tracks by the sight of two warriors, swaying dangerously as they fought together on top of the wall.

Cleopas held his breath. With an anguished cry, one of the men clawed at the air for a moment, and then fell. He hit the ground with a thud. Blood gushed out from a wound in his chest. Cleopas raced across the square and squatted down beside the twisted form. Ompu Tinggi's man. He was dead. Cleopas crouched there, his arm round the dead man's shoulder, looking up at the wall. He wanted to cry out, but his tongue was leaden and he could not speak.

With a great scream of fury, Ompu Tinggi raged past him and leaped up on to the wall, brandishing his knife. "Come on! Come on! We'll get you! By all the gods and spirits we'll get you!"

The men of the village gave an angry roar and stampeded after him, yelling out threats of revenge. The attackers turned and fled.

Carefully Cleopas laid the victim on the ground. Then he jumped up and ran to climb the wall.

He caught up with the Lumban Bagasan army on an open stretch of ground not far from the village. He rushed up to where Ompu Tinggi stood deep in talk with his chief fighters.

"Please, Ompu," he gasped, catching hold of the raja's arm. "Stop this fighting!" He paused to catch his breath. "Let them go! What's more important now is to take care of the wounded, and to bury the dead."

The raja stood stiffly, without speaking.

"Please, Ompu. If this fighting goes on it will only lead to more people being killed."

The raja frowned down at the ground for a moment, and then looked slowly round the circle of his men. No one spoke. The young Bataks grasped their weapons tightly, watching and waiting. Tinggi stared into the teacher's face. Then he gave a deep sigh.

"You're right, Cleopas," he said, as the teacher released his arm. "Very well." He nodded to his troops. "Come on then. We'll all go home."

The war was over — for a while.

Attitudes were changing. Ompu Tinggi began to study the Christian faith in earnest, and soon others were asking to join the catechism classes, both in Lumban Bagasan and in the surrounding countryside. In December Bishop Nommensen paid them a visit, and baptized their first converts — 125 people, including Ompu Tinggi himself and his family.

"Wonderful," enthused Nommensen as they ate together after the service. "My friends in Germany are praying for you, you know, Cleopas. I shall write now and tell them we have some firstfruits."

Petronella was cooking, with a team of women from the village. She paused a moment in ladling out rice, and glanced across to where the bishop was deep in conversation with her husband. So much had happened since that February day when he had blessed them and sent them out! She straightened her aching back and gave a small sigh. Her neighbour looked sharply at her.

"It's time you rested now," she said sternly. "Go and sit down over there," gesturing with her chin to a shady corner. "My daughter can do that."

"Yes, mm, yes," murmured Petronella, looking round vaguely.

"You need to be careful now," said the older woman, with a meaning glance at Petronella's stomach. "Won't be long now."

"No it won't," sighed Petronella as she dragged her unwieldy body over to the corner. If only the bishop would take her back with him when he left tomorrow. She wondered if she dare suggest such a thing. The thought of giving birth to her first baby so far from home filled her with terror.

Carefully she eased herself down on to the rattan mat. Her ankles were swollen and she felt breathless. There were so many things that she should have asked her mother, or her sisters; so many things she didn't know.

"Don't worry." The woman sitting beside her patted her knee as if in answer. She held a baby at her breast, and another child was scrabbling by her feet. She looked superbly confident as she smiled at Petronella. "We'll take care of you."

A few days later Cleopas returned from his visiting rounds to find three girls sitting outside his house.

"You can't go up, Teacher," said the eldest, whom he recognized as one of the raja's daughters. "We're waiting here to take messages. Your wife is going to have her baby."

"My wife!" Cleopas bounded up the short ladder.

"Go away, Teacher Cleopas. You mustn't come in now!"

In the dusky light it seemed as if a thousand women were thronging to and fro. He thought he could just make out his wife, crouching down in a corner.

"Boru Pohan-Simanjuntak?"

"Go away," said Petronella.

"Are you all right?"

"Go away, Teacher," commanded the raja's wife. "You know that men are not allowed in the house when a baby is to be born. You must go immediately and talk to the father of my children."

Petronella gave a moan. Cleopas turned pale and backed down the steps.

Towards midnight on Christmas Eve, 1885, the Lord blessed the Lumbantobings with their first child, a son.

It was a turning point for Petronella. The women of the village had taken charge of the whole event, in place of the family she was missing so much. She was one of them now — a fully fledged adult woman, the mother of a son. Their kindness to her, and her own joy in her tiny new baby, made life in Lumban Bagasan Toba suddenly bearable.

The young girls bustled round, taking care of all the household tasks while she rested against the fire. Ompu Tinggi's wife shouted her directions as imperiously as Petronella's mother-in-law would have done if they had been living in their own village. The placenta must go under the house there; the young mother must roast herself against the fire for a week, here; the baby must be draped in an ulos (shawl) so; and on the eighth day he must be taken to the river to be washed. The mother must choose a name for the child.

"Samuel," murmured Petronella weakly.

Cleopas hovered on the outskirts, tossing in his comments and opinions.

"You can't do that!" he protested, when he found two girls digging a hole under the house shortly after the birth, to bury the placenta.

"But we have to, Teacher. Some of the baby's tondi is in here, its soul stuff."

"No!" said Cleopas firmly. "We don't believe that." Nommensen had allowed many adat practices, but had always been resolute in opposing the tondi-cult. A person's "tondi" was regarded as something akin to the soul, but more loosely attached, and with an identity of its own. If annoyed, it might leave him for good, and the person would die. Babies were especially vulnerable, as the soft fontanelle on their heads made an easy exit point for the fickle tondi.

"The 'younger brother' must be buried here," said the raja's wife, appearing suddenly at the sound of voices. "Otherwise your baby will get sick and die."

"We are Christians, Aunt," said Cleopas. "And so are you now. We believe that God is the one who protects us and our children. We don't fear the spirits any more."

They faced each other in the flickering light of the banana wood torches. Cleopas had taught the Toba Bataks so much, over the past months, about the great High God who loved them and had sent His Son; and about the power of Jesus Christ, who could free them from bondage to evil spirits. They had promised, at their baptism, to believe and trust in Jesus. But must they deliberately flout all the traditions of their ancestors?

"Yes, Teacher," said the raja's wife in polite agreement. "But if we don't bury it, then a datu might come and steal it for his magic spells."

Cleopas frowned. On every side, it seemed, the old beliefs pressed in, and the demons lurked ready to snatch away the fragile faith of his new Christians.

"Bury it, then," he said. "But as Christians we don't attach any significance to it. None at all."

It was Christmas Day already. He must preach to them the Christmas message — explain again the meaning of Christ become flesh and blood and convince them that those who believe in Jesus need fear no evil. He sighed. Over a hundred new believers, but there was still so much they needed to learn about the Christian faith.

Cleopas's ministry grew steadily over the next two years, with regular services and catechism classes in all the surrounding villages.

"We need more workers," he wrote to Nommensen.

"Look to the Christians you have there," was the bishop's initial response. "Use them in the work, and watch for those who could be trained as Bible teachers."

Cleopas picked out from each group a number who showed potential. He tried to involve them in his ministry of teaching and visiting, and in decision making. He set aside time each week to give them a more thorough grounding in the basics of Christianity. They would be the elders of the new churches.

On December 21, 1887, Bishop Nommensen visited Lumban Bagasan Toba again, this time for a service of consecration. The mission posts in six villages were commissioned as independent congregations, just two years after the first baptisms. A Bible teacher was to be appointed to serve in each one.

"Your teacher Cleopas has finished his work here," said the bishop in his sermon. "Each new adult congregation will have its own teacher. Cleopas has planted, and now other workers will tend the young shoots." He smiled at Cleopas. "So now I'm calling him back to Silindung, so that he can do further studies and be ordained as a pendeta."

Petronella looked up from her place at the back of the church. Baby Frederick, just three weeks old, lay snugly in his shawl against her breast. Samuel was outside somewhere in the care of one of the village girls. The two children had done much to reconcile Petronella to living in Toba. It would be hard to leave.

"But we are not really parting," declared Ompu Tinggi, in his farewell speech. "We shan't be separated, because we are one in

Christ. Even though we do not see each other, we remain united. We are still one. May the Lord lead and direct our steps for his glory."

Nommensen's vision was for an independent Batak Church served by national ordained ministers. It was a vision shared by most missionaries, perhaps, in most mission fields. But in practice nineteenth-century paternalism and conscious or unconscious feelings of racial superiority slowed the process down considerably. In Sumatra, however, the Church was mushrooming at such an amazing rate that it was quite impossible to provide all the workers needed from Europe. In 1871 the baptized Christians numbered 1,250. By 1881 the figure had risen to 5,988, and by 1891 it was 21,779. This was God's harvest time for Batakland, Nommensen felt, and it was essential to train Batak Christians to share the work of reaping.

In March 1884 the school at Pansur Napitu had been expanded to include a seminary where trained and experienced Bible teachers could take a short upgrading course leading to ordination. Cleopas was one of six students to start the course at the end of December 1887.

As there was no accommodation for families at the school, wives and children had to be left behind. Petronella stayed with the two little boys at her mother-in-law's house in Pulopulo II. As the village was within walking distance of the seminary, Cleopas could visit his family often.

Cleopas had served the Lord for four years now as a Bible and school teacher. He had seen the power of God at work, even in small details of his life, and his trust had deepened as he experienced many answers to prayer. But increasingly he had felt aware of his own ignorance, and he was grateful for the opportunity to study.

Especially valuable were the many discussions with his fellow-students, as they talked through the problems they had encountered in their ministry.

How could they explain the gospel so that it pierced through the prejudices of their hearers? How should they deal with violence and jealousies? How could they lead on those who trembled at the brink, who longed to believe, but were too afraid to say no to the old ways? And what of those who accepted Christ, but who clung to the old beliefs too? Some traditions were good and should be maintained, but there was much in their adat that was inextricably linked with spirit worship. How could they discern which was which?

The six new ministers were ordained on August 10, 1889. A group of elders came to the service from Lumban Bagasan Toba, led by Raja Polin, the son of Ompu Tinggi, who had recently died. Polin been a good friend to Cleopas and his family during their time at Lumban Bagasan, and he was anxious that the new minister should return to work among them. Nommensen agreed.

The Lumbantobing family set off on September 1, with newly born baby Lucius wrapped in a sling. As before, they stopped for a few days at Laguboti. Nommensen himself was living there now, dividing his time between Lake Toba and Silindung. He had much to tell them about the progress of the gospel in that region during the past two years.

The news soon spread of their arrival, and a great crowd came from Lumban Bagasan Toba to escort them on the last stage of their journey.

Cleopas smiled at his wife as she carefully unwrapped her new baby and handed him over to a young Toba girl. All around them willing helpers were taking charge of their baggage, exclaiming over the height, good health and sure intelligence of the two older boys, and praising God's goodness in granting them three fine sons.

"I am determined," he murmured, "to do everything I can to work for the good of these people and the glory of God. Agreed?"

Petronella nodded, smiling. This was a homecoming to be proud of.

AGAINST THE SPIRITUAL FORCES OF EVIL 8

Raja Polin was waiting to greet Cleopas and his family at Lumban Bagasan Toba. Their house had been swept and made ready and a special meal cooked for them all to share. As they ate, Polin told Cleopas of his plans to build a church.

"A church building, you mean, here in Lumban Bagasan?" Cleopas nodded thoughtfully. Until now they had been using the sopo, the large rice barn which doubled as a village meeting-place. "That would be wonderful! Just one problem. I'm not sure how much money would be available just now from the Church office in Pearaja."

"No problem," said Polin. "Don't worry. I know there are many, many people who want to help."

"I'll tell the bishop when I see him next."

Nommensen was delighted, not least because the suggestion had come from the raja himself. The church building project started early in 1890. The Church office sent a donation to help, and Raja Polin organized teams of workers to collect building materials. They were sent off in groups into the forest; some to fell the tall trees, others to chop up the trunks into manageable proportions, while other groups hand-sawed them into planks and boards, or carried the prepared wood to the building site.

The raja's enthusiasm was infectious, and soon not only the Christians but many who still worshipped the spirits were working away in a remarkable spirit of unity. At the consecration service eight months later, Cleopas praised God that the building had been completed with no fights or quarrels, no raised voices, and no accidents. The smooth teamwork had been a witness to God's grace, no less than the beauty of the finished building.

But if the Bataks of Lumban Bagasan Toba were learning to live together in peace, it was very different in the surrounding countryside. Many had been so impressed by the church building that they began to come along to the Sunday services. But in their belts they carried hidden daggers, and some brought guns.

Often, after the service, a fight would break out in the church-yard. This was one of the few times when members of rival villages or factions came face to face, sometimes after days of watching each other warily from a distance. A hasty word or an angry glance, and the tense atmosphere would erupt at once into vio-lence. More than once Cleopas leaped into the middle of an ugly crowd, with scant regard for his own safety, to soothe or rebuke the combatants. They would turn away, ashamed, with a muttered excuse, only to be at each others' throats again the following Sunday.

"That's what makes us Bataks," explained Raja Polin one day. "Our fighting spirit. Our aggression. Our manliness. Our deter-mination to take our proper place; to hold on to what we own and to take revenge if anyone wrongs us. It's all part of being a Batak."

"Yes, I know," sighed Cleopas. "But I'm sure it doesn't have to be that way. It's good to be bold and strong, but couldn't we be strong for God's glory, instead of our own? It's good to make peace too. Why, a good part of our adat traditions are to do with different ways of making peace!"

"Ah yes," laughed Polin, "but isn't that because we spend so much of our time making war! Anyway, Cleopas, I'm sure that you've been doing all you can as a peacemaker."

They were at the pendeta's house with a group of elders prepar-ing a church report for Bishop Nommensen, who was holding a visitation at Laguboti.

"I've been doing what I can," agreed Cleopas. "Samuel's

mother and I spend a lot of time visiting in the villages round here. Whenever I get the chance I tell them how Jesus came as a peacemaker, to reconcile us to God and to each other. I try to explain to them what Christian love is all about and how we need to forgive."

"That's the hard part," said Polin, "— the forgiving."

"And the datus make it harder, Ompu," added one of the elders. "They don't like your gospel of peace, Pendeta. It threatens their power. The datus are the ones with the magic power people need to get revenge: to spoil the enemy's crops, or to make him fall sick or his children die. They don't like your telling people to love their enemy."

"It's the datus who keep stirring up warfare between villages," put in another elder. "I'm sure of it."

Cleopas sighed again. He had been trying hard to break the deadlock between two villages, Pangaribuan and Pintu Bosi, which had long been at loggerheads. Neither side would budge an inch and neither showed any interest in the Christian faith.

"Are we ready, then?" Polin tapped the account books in front of him.

"Yes, let's go," said Cleopas. "The bishop will be waiting."

They were just setting off when a young Batak stumbled through the narrow gateway to the village and sank exhausted on the ground.

"Pendeta Cleopas!" he gasped.

"What's the matter? Where have you come from?" said Polin.

"Pintu Bosi." The young man struggled for breath. "We've been attacked!"

"By Pangaribuan," breathed Cleopas.

The man nodded. "They've stuck up a magic staff — pangu-labalang. We'll all be killed!"

The elders looked at him in horror. Batak wars, although frequent, were usually limited affairs in which the first injuries indicated guilt or innocence, and quickly led to peace. But the pangulabalang meant a declaration of war to the death.

Each Batak clan had a magic staff — a wooden stick up to two metres long, elaborately carved with mythical figures. The staff, usually kept by the datu, had a hollow centre, into which was poured a special substance known as pupuk.

Pupuk was obtained by kidnapping a small boy, about three years old, from a hostile village. He was kept for a year as a privileged guest, well fed and entertained, and occasionally treated to a drink of palm wine from a buffalo horn.

After about a year the child would be asked, "Will you go where we send you and defeat our enemies?"

If he said yes he was led out of the village and placed in a deep hole with only his head above ground.

"Will you allow yourself to be sent by me?" the datu would ask him again.

"Yes of course," the unsuspecting child would agree, and the datu would hand him the drinking horn. Molten lead would be poured into his mouth and he would die quickly and in great pain.

The child's body would then be used to prepare the pupuk, which was divided out for various magic purposes but chiefly to be used in the magic staff. His tondi, or soul-stuff, which remained in contact with the body, was bound by the promise made before death and would fight for the clan against their enemies.

This magic staff stuck in the ground at the entrance to Pintu Bosi was more than a declaration of war. It was a sign that anyone coming out of the village would surely die, and that soon the village itself would be attacked and burned to the ground. The villagers would all be killed unless they surrendered immediately, in which case they would be taken as slaves.

"We've strengthened the entrance and the walls," said the young Batak. "The women and children are all safe, hiding in their houses, and the men are on guard, waiting. I managed to get out and came running to tell the pendeta."

"I must go there at once," said Cleopas.

"To Pintu Bosi? Right into the battlefield?" The elders looked at him aghast.

"Yes, to Pintu Bosi."

"No, you can't, Pendeta! You mustn't!"

"It's too late," said Polin. "There's no room for a peacemaker now if they've stuck that thing up. If you go now you'll only be killed."

"The raja's right, Pendeta," said one of the older men. His hand shook as he waved it in the general direction of Pintu Bosi. "All that area is a battlefield now. It's too dangerous."

"But I'm not going to fight," said Cleopas gently. "I'm going to ask them to make peace."

"Ah, Pendeta, knives and bullets don't recognize ministers of the gospel." The old man clutched Cleopas's arm, shaking his head sorrowfully. "These are wild men, Pendeta, men who've been bewitched! What do they care about peace?"

"Yes, I know, but even so, it's my duty to bring peace to them — to those very places which are in the grip of hatred and war." He patted the elder's hand. "I must do the will of Jesus Christ who sent me here. That's why I have to go."

Before anyone could protest further he asked them to join him in prayer. "You may be sure I shall not go alone," he reminded them. "The Lord will be with me and He's greater than all the spirits."

Cleopas would allow none of the elders from Lumban Bagasan Toba to go with him. But they exchanged glances after he left, and then turned with one accord to follow Cleopas and the messenger at a discreet distance.

"There are evil forces at work," said Raja Polin. "And you never know when we may be needed."

The country was wide and flat here, at the southern edge of Lake Toba, and Cleopas could see from some distance away the sturdy bamboo thicket surrounding Pintu Bosi. He followed the road round the lakeside, almost to Laguboti, then turned off abruptly along a narrow track leading straight through the paddyfields.

As they drew near he could hear quite clearly the shouted taunts and insults of the beseiging army, gathered in force on a piece of open ground in front of the village. The men fell silent as he approached, and stood watching to see what he would do. The elders from Lumban Bagasan Toba quickened their steps, so that they had almost caught up with him when he came in sight of the magic staff.

Cleopas stopped.

The black carved staff stood erect like a flagpole, right in front of the gateway to Pintu Bosi. Long green leaves sprouted like a feathered headdress from its top, tied in place by a three-stranded thread of red, black and white. An array of charms, pieces of bamboo, small knives and human skulls jangled hollowly as they swayed together in the soft breeze. The datu of Pangaribuan had strengthened the pangulabalang spirit in his staff by adding as many occult powers as he could command.

Cleopas stood as if frozen, staring at the staff. He was only too well aware what it signified.

No one spoke. No one moved. Evil powers were at work here, and every Batak stood in awe of them.

All eyes were on Cleopas. Suddenly they saw him gasp and blink, then blink again. His eyes widened, and he took a step forward. The men from Pangaribuan, the watchers on the village wall, the elders from Lumban Bagasan Toba, all stood transfixed as Cleopas walked slowly but steadily up to the gateway of Pintu Bosi. His gaze was fixed unwaveringly on some point above and beyond the magic staff.

As Cleopas approached the staff, he slipped his ulos, the special Batak shawl, from his shoulders. With both hands he held it up above his head, waving it from side to side in a gesture of peace.

"Stop, in the name of the Lord," he called as he went. "Stop your fighting! God wants you to make peace!" He turned round to face the beseiging army, still waving the ulos above his head.

"God the Father of our Lord Jesus Christ wants you to make peace."

Slinging the ulos over his shoulder, he grasped hold of the staff with both hands and wrenched it out of the ground. He held it up so that all could see. "Honoured rajas!" he cried, pointing the staff up towards the wall, and then turning again to face the attackers, "Honoured rajas! Brothers! The staff has been pulled up! Stop your warfare!"

One by one he unfastened the sacred objects hanging from the staff — the skulls, knives, magic cloths, pieces of bamboo on which were scratched spells and curses, everything which gave the staff its awesome power. He pulled them off piece by piece and tossed them in a pile on the ground.

The silence was thick and heavy with the smell of fear. Both armies had watched astounded as Cleopas uprooted the magic staff. But when he began to pull off the death spells they were terror-stricken. The men of Pintu Bosi crouched low on their wall. Slowly the Pangaribuan soldiers backed away, afraid that they too would suffer the revenge of their guardian spirit who was being so humiliated. But their feet were like lead, and their eyes were caught, like those of a petrified animal facing its attacker.

No one dared to fire a weapon; no one dared to cry out. They waited in mounting horror for the spirit in the staff to destroy this man who showed such contempt. They could not believe that the man who had pulled up the staff could stand there slowly stripping it of all its trappings, and suffer no harm.

Cleopas took the naked staff and stuck it back in the ground. Then he called to the leaders of both armies to come up and make peace.

No one stirred. Cleopas waited silently, looking around the open ground, glancing up at the wall behind him, hoping that someone would come forward. Not a whisper could be heard. Mouths gaped, eyes stared. They were waiting, still, for the spirit to strike Cleopas dead.

Nothing happened.

"Elders, honoured rajas!" his voice rang out again. "Come, let's make peace." He took a deep breath.

Silence. No one was going to be so foolish as to go near a spirit who had been completely humiliated and would certainly rage with fury.

Eventually the Raja of Pangaribuan got to his feet. Cleopas rushed over immediately, grabbed him by the hand, and almost dragged him across the open ground to the staff.

"Ompu," he pleaded, "if these wars go on and on, how can we ever hope to make this region safe and prosperous? When will there be an end to this hatred — this constant lust for revenge?"

The raja only shook his head, but he went with Cleopas, right up to the pangulabalang staff.

"Bishop Nommensen has been praying for peace in this district for years now," said Cleopas. "Would you like to meet him?"

"Where is he?"

"He's at Laguboti. He's waiting for us there ... How long are you going to let him go on waiting?"

Cleopas broke off when he saw the raja of Pintu Bosi coming out through the narrow gateway. He grasped the raja's hand, and brought him across to meet his enemy.

Seeing their leaders face to face, the commanders from both armies came up to join them, together with the church elders from Lumban Bagasan Toba. Cleopas beamed at them all.

"How wonderful it would be," he said, "if we could all live together in peace and harmony as neighbours and brothers, loving one another!"

The sudden release of tension was like a dam bursting. With hoots of laughter, the people of Pintu Bosi rushed about their tasks, preparing an enormous peace feast. Several pigs and a buffalo were slaughtered. They sang and danced and made riddles and jokes, and a few of the soldiers fenced together lightheartedly, while a laughing audience cheered them on.

The two rajas agreed that any future disagreements would be

settled through the mediation of Cleopas. As a guarantee of peace, they each presented him with a ring and a sword, to be given to the bishop.

"Why not come with me now," he suggested. "We can take these tokens to Bishop Nommensen right now."

After the feast the rajas and leading men from both villages went with Cleopas and his friends to Laguboti. Nommensen was delighted to see them, and to receive from their hands the rings and swords which were to be binding tokens of peace. He reminded them of the many benefits they would enjoy if they learned to live together in harmony, and told them that God could give them peace if they would trust in Him.

It was late that night when Cleopas and the church elders set off back along the road to Lumban Bagasan Toba.

"Pendeta Cleopas," said one of the elders as they walked along beside the lake, "what was it that made you look so astonished, back there at Pintu Bosi? You seemed to be staring at something — but it wasn't just the magic staff."

"Oh! We're forgetting!" Cleopas stopped suddenly, his face dejected. "We forgot to thank the Lord!" He stood for a moment, looking back through the dark in the direction of Pintu Bosi. "How could we do such a thing! We ate a huge feast, and made many speeches, and called out 'Horas!' to each other like the good Bataks we are. But we forgot to give thanks to God for His help and protection!" He was clearly very perturbed.

"What was it you saw?" asked Polin, thinking to take his mind off his shortcomings.

"To be honest with you," said Cleopas, "I was absolutely terrified when I saw that staff. We all know what it means when the spirit is set to guard the entrance to a village like that. All the forces of evil were arrayed against us. And in spite of all I've been teaching you about the power of the Lord being stronger, I was so full of fear that I didn't know what to do."

He paused, and the others nodded their sympathy.

"But then, all at once, I saw a cross, quite clearly, shining out above and behind the staff. The cross of Jesus. It was so bright I was dazzled! I saw it there for just a moment, and then it vanished. But it gave me courage. That's how I knew for certain that God was with me."

THE HOSTAGE 9

The peace was barely two weeks old when the datu of Pangaribuan began to stir up trouble. He complained that they had been tricked by the Dutch East India Company. In fact, he said, the Pangaribuan army had already defeated Pintu Bosi. All that remained was to press on and destroy them completely, especially since they had clearly been plotting with that white man, Nommensen.

The datu of Pintu Bosi was outraged when he heard this, and he challenged his rival to a dual one market day.

Crowds from both villages gathered round. The datus first yelled insults at each other, and then began a trial of skill. One datu took some poison and sent it flying through the air. The other caught it and stuffed it into a long red chilli, which he wore as an earring to show his immunity from his opponent's power.

Their supporters became more and more excited, shouting and screaming and calling out names. They were spoiling for a fight, but both sides felt bound by the promises given to Nommensen. Tempers were high when the crowds dispersed towards evening.

That night the raja of Pangaribuan stormed off to Lumban Bagasan Toba with a group of his followers and demanded the return of his sword and ring. Cleopas was dismayed when he heard what had happened. He tried to calm the raja down, explaining that he no longer had the guarantees of peace and so could not possibly return them.

All his explanations were brushed aside. Although the raja had seen with his own eyes the presentation of the rings and swords to Bishop Nommensen in Laguboti, he insisted that the minister should give him back his guarantees immediately.

"You took them, Pendeta!" he shouted, "You received them from our hands, and we want them back now! Right now, this minute!"

Hearing the uproar at the minister's house, Raja Polin came down from his own house nearby.

"Honoured raja," he said in measured tones. "If you insist that the pendeta must return those guarantees to you this very night, then he will have to go to Laguboti to ask for them. Then Bishop Nommensen will know that you have all come here in the middle of the night, disturbing Pendeta Cleopas. And don't forget there's a Dutch garrison at Laguboti now. If the Company hears of this, they'll think you're starting a riot! This very night the troops will be sent out to arrest you!"

Polin looked sternly at the raja of Pangaribuan, who was shaking his head in dismay.

"Not only that," he added. "But weren't those guarantees given to a raja? Be careful you don't violate Batak adat. Our pendeta here is the son of a raja held in great respect in Silindung valley. If that raja hears that the raja of Pangaribuan has humiliated his son, won't he be angry? He will march against you with his army and bring the Dutch soldiers with him!" He paused. "And if that happens then we ourselves will be forced to fight against Pangaribuan, because we are allies of that raja."

Polin stood with his arms folded and his head erect. The men from Pangaribuan looked at him in some bewilderment. They had not thought so far ahead. They had come quickly in the heat of their anger, and they had never considered that the consequences might be so far-reaching.

The raja stood stiffly, clinging to the vestiges of his authority.

"Come to my house," said Polin. "Come and drink coffee with me, to warm you all up, before you walk home in this cold night air."

Cleopas told Nommensen what had happened a few days later. He felt very dejected.

"Yes, it is disappointing," agreed the bishop.

"And what's even worse," added Cleopas, "everywhere I go people are talking about how I persuaded Pangaribuan and Pintu Bosi to make peace! But they are not talking about the peace-making. Not the gospel. Not the message I brought them of peace and love. It's how brave I was, and how powerful I must be to go up to that magic staff and strip it bare and throw it down." He shook his head. "They're saying I must have some secret power that's even greater than the pangulabalang spirit."

"Occult power, you mean, that comes from the spirits?"

Cleopas nodded sadly. "I'd rejoice if they were saying it's the power of the God I'm preaching about." He sighed. "It's not the Christians who are saying those things, of course. But I realize now something of what the Lord Jesus must have felt when the Pharisees accused him of casting out demons by the power of Satan."

"Don't be afraid," said Nommensen. "Never forget that the Lord is with us. We know that He is the One who gives victory. They'll see it one day."

Shortly after this news came of warfare between the villages of Janjimaria and Parsambilan. In a sudden attack, the army from Janjimaria had taken hostage a young girl from Parsambilan. They put her in the stocks under their raja's house, waiting for the pro-pitious time to kill and eat her. They strengthened the fortifica-tions round their village in case of a revenge attack.

The people of Parsambilan were panic-stricken. All the men gathered in the sopo, and they spent a day and a night in deep discussion, trying to decide on a strategy of war. They were terri-fied of making a wrong move.

The Bataks often took hostages. Such prisoners might be held for years, with one ankle firmly secured by a wooden plank to a heavy stone block. Unable properly to sit, stand or lie down, they would be alone with the pigs penned each night in the dark shelter under the house. But sometimes — especially under provo-cation — the prisoner might be killed and eaten at a special feast.

At first light came news that the cymbals were sounding in Janjimaria, inviting their people in the surrounding countryside to come to a feast.

While the leaders of Parsambilan had been holding their meet-ing, some Christians from a neighbouring village had sent word of the disaster to Nommensen. Nommensen and Cleopas had talked with the leaders in both places, some of whom knew Cleopas's family. But both had so far been hostile to the Christian faith.

The bishop wrote a letter to Cleopas, asking him to go at once to Janjimaria with Raja Polin. He hoped that the raja's authority would be accepted by both sides.

Nommensen gave the messenger his umbrella to pass on to Cleopas. This had long been an object of awe and veneration to the Bataks, who perhaps equated it with a datu's staff. If Cleopas opened the umbrella over the hostage, wrote Nommensen, this would symbolize the bishop's protection of the girl. He himself would follow them to Janjimaria as soon as possible.

Cleopas and Polin set off that night, and reached Janjimaria as light dawned, in time to hear the cymbals clashing to announce the feast.

The young girl had already been brought out from the stocks and tied to a stake in the middle of the village square. Fires were alight nearby, and women were busy pounding chillies and spices. Lemons and salt were ready. The datu had cut off the girl's hair, rich in soulstuff power, to make his medicines. The raja was just slicing off her ears when a watchman on the wall cried out a warning that two men were hurrying along the track towards the village.

The raja ordered his soldiers to prepare for battle. The hostage, blood streaming from her face, was quickly cut down from the stake and rolled up in a rattan mat. In a few moments the square was filled with soldiers armed with knives and rifles. The guard stood at his post on the wall.

"We've come to speak with the head of your village," came a cry from outside the gate. "Stop your preparations, please, and stop your feasting. We want to talk to the raja."

"Oh, it's Pendeta Cleopas, is it?" called the guard. "And what right have you to come to our village, interfering with our feast? It's none of your business, and you might as well know that whatever you do you can't stop us now!"

For several minutes Cleopas and Polin waited outside the gate. Eventually the raja gave permission for them to enter and they were led to the large square. Out of sight underneath the raja's house lay the young hostage, rolled up in the rattan mat. She had no strength left to cry out.

The raja, surrounded by his nobles and soldiers, stood facing the newcomers. The women and children gathered round to listen. Cleopas spoke out clearly so that all could hear. He told them of God's love for them all, and of his own love and his desire to bring peace in the Toba region. He pleaded with them to take pity on the young girl and let her go. But their anger was like a hard wall, shutting out his words.

"That girl is *our* hostage. *Ours!*" said one of the nobles firmly. "We can do what we like with her. She belongs to us now."

Before Cleopas could reply, a young man of about his own age stepped forward.

"Who are you, then?" he jeered, stabbing his finger in the air as he came up to Cleopas and walked slowly round him. "Who do you think you are that we should have to listen to all your talk?"

He glared at the pendeta, fingering the dagger at his belt as he talked. There were growls of encouragement from the crowd. Cleopas ignored him and spoke directly to the raja.

"Ompu, we came here to beg for your pity. Not — certainly not ..."

"Stop that begging!" snarled the soldier. "Answer my question!"

Cleopas drew himself up to his full height.

"How is this, honoured raja, son of Janjinausangan?" he said in a quiet but dignified voice, taking no notice of the soldier who stood sneering in front of him. "We come to speak with you as fellow rajas, and I come also as your pastor. I am a child of Ompu Patia and son of Raja Solomon of Silindung, and I come here with Raja Polin, the Raja of Lumban Bagasan Toba. Is this how you welcome rajas here?" He looked round the square in disapproval. "No mat has been rolled out on the ground, so that your visitors and fellow rajas might have a place to sit. And yet the one who comes is the child of your friend and teacher!"

There was a shocked silence. Everyone was taken aback by the rebuke.

"What! The son of our friends?"

"A child of the great datu?"

"But we didn't realize."

The murmurs ran through the crowd of old men like ripples across a pool. The soldier who had snapped at Cleopas turned away in confusion.

Cleopas bent his head wearily. He was aware that if the situation had changed it was because of his kinship with a famous datu, a man who could tap the powers of evil, and not because he was a minister of peace.

The raja of Janjimaria was ashamed. He had commited a serious offence against Batak adat and had lost face. With a snap of his fingers he sent his servants running to fetch a large mat, which was rolled out on the square. He gestured to his guests to sit down. In a long and elaborate speech he apologized for his failure to recognize the son of his friend and teacher, and the Raja of Lumban Bagasan Toba, and for neglecting to show them the respect and attention they deserved.

"Yes, it's true that Ompu Patia is our friend and teacher," he acknowledged. "He even entrusted his horses to us."

Cleopas explained that Ompu Patia was his uncle, the younger brother of his father Ompu Ginjang, or Raja Solomon as he was now called. The change of name gave the opportunity to explain what it meant to become a Christian, and to be born again into the Christian family. Cleopas told them about the laws of God, who created the world and everything in it, and His purposes of love for mankind. More and more people gathered round to listen as he talked.

The raja of Janjimaria listened carefully, and seemed to understand the gospel message. He made no protest when Cleopas returned again to the immediate purpose of their visit and asked them once more to spare the girl's life.

Several of the older men seemed sympathetic. But some of the leaders, backed by the young soldiers, were determined to press on with the feast. The raja looked round their faces with heavy eyes. He was caught in a cleft stick. Whichever answer he gave he would lose face.

"Horas!"

Everyone looked round in astonishment, to see Bishop Nommensen standing at the entrance to the village.

"Horas!" he cried again, in the traditional Batak greeting.

The Bataks sprang to their feet in consternation.

"Horas!"

The raja leaped forward to welcome the bishop, and led him to a place on the mat next to his own. Nommensen listened carefully as Cleopas told him all that had been discussed, and then he spoke.

"My brothers," he said. "Just try to imagine how you would feel if your own child, your own son or daughter, was captured and tortured like this young girl you have taken." He was looking round as he spoke, trying to see the hostage. The stake was there in the middle of the square, but the victim was nowhere in sight. "So foolish, wanting to eat people," he added. "Won't you be eating your own children one day?"

No one spoke. Nommensen stood up and turned round, trying

to make out where the girl was hidden. As he peered through the wooden bars under the raja's house his eyes lit suddenly on a roll of bloodstained matting. He turned back to face the crowd.

"God's Word teaches us to love our neighbour," he said. "Won't you let me take this human being and give you a buffalo to eat in exchange? Buffalo meat is far better than human flesh."

Catching Cleopas's eye, the bishop turned and walked over to the raja's house, stooping a little to look underneath. Cleopas and Polin followed him as he stepped through the bars and crossed to the bundle of matting. With an embarrassed murmur the raja and his nobles joined them. Other villagers crowded round the house, talking together in low voices, wondering what would happen.

Nommensen and Cleopas squatted on the ground. With fumbling fingers they untied the ropes and gently unrolled the matting. They stared at each other in sick horror when they saw the girl. Her ears had been cut off. Flies were buzzing sleepily around the bloody mess of her head. She was unconscious, but as Nommensen touched her forehead her eyelids quivered slightly. She gave a moan and then fainted again.

"Cloths," said Nommensen sharply. "Bring cloths and some boiling water! Quickly!"

Some of the women ran to fetch water. Gently Nommensen bathed her face and tended her wounds. Cleopas held the bowl, replacing it again and again with fresh water. He could hardly bear to look at the victim. She was only about eighteen years old, and had perhaps been beautiful.

"Here's some money," said Nommensen in a low voice to Polin. "See if you can organize a buffalo for them to feast on instead."

As they waited for the girl to regain consciousness, Nommensen and Cleopas again begged the raja to allow them to take her home to her parents. Raja Polin returned with a waterbuffalo, and the bishop made a very solemn speech, handing over the animal as a ransom for the hostage and a thank-offering for the whole village to share. Only then did the captors agree to release the girl.

As the bishop and his envoys carried her away they could hear the shouts of joy and triumph as the people of Janjimaria prepared to slaughter their fat buffalo.

The news went ahead of them to Parsambilan, and huge crowds streamed out of the village to meet them. The girl's family hugged and kissed her again and again, weeping over her injuries but rejoicing that she had been rescued from a worse fate. Grains of rice were sprinkled over her head, and over the bishop and his two envoys, in the traditional sign of welcome and honour. Over and over again the family thanked the three men for all they had done, pressing them to stay for a celebration feast.

Before they ate, Nommensen asked for permission to speak.

"I want to ask you something very hard," he said. "Something which you can only do with God's help. By God's mercy your daughter has been returned to you. And I want to beg you all now to forgive those who have wronged you." He looked at the girl's father. "They *have* wronged you, I know. Very badly. But please don't hold bitterness in your hearts, and don't seek revenge. Just thank God for giving you back your daughter."

There was a long pause before the raja rose to reply.

After thanking Nommensen and the others for rescuing the young hostage, he went on, "We know what you mean — we don't want any more fighting. We will remember. And we hope that you'll come often to visit us."

The leading men of the village murmured their agreement and promised that in future, if disputes arose, they would call on the bishop and his helpers to help find a peaceful settlement.

Over the following months Cleopas paid many visits to Parsambilan, holding services and catechism classes. During the first year more than twenty people confessed their faith in Jesus Christ as their Lord and Saviour. Cleopas rejoiced to see the fruits of the gospel in the daily lives of the villagers.

"It's not that they *never* get angry or start fighting," he explained to Nommensen. "But I don't see long-drawn-out feuds now in

Parsambilan. If a quarrel does break out, then they settle it themselves quickly, without any need to call on me or Raja Polin."

"You see!" said the bishop. "It's as I told you before. The Lord *is* with us. It takes time and patience. But the Lord is at work, and He is able to bring peace, even here."

THE GOSPEL OF PEACE 10

The Dutch Controller stretched out his legs and shrugged his shoulders in a gesture of despair.

"I'm at my wit's end," he said. "But I don't want to involve you in all my problems, Bishop Nommensen. I simply came as a matter of respect, to ask your opinion as head of the Church here, before I make a final decision."

Nommensen nodded politely. His mind had been racing since the moment van Dijk arrived at his house in Sigumpar.

"Of course we always do have fighting in the Toba region," continued the Dutch officer. "It's a constant headache, though often a minor one." He gave a short bark of a laugh. "My soldiers watch them at it sometimes, from the garrison. You wouldn't believe the ammunition they get through — but the enemy don't get hit much. Ha!" Another bark. "But this war now in Laguboti, between these two clans, Hasibuan and Manurung. This time it's got beyond a joke."

"Yes, I know."

"The Hasibuan are bent on out-and out destruction. They've got the Manurung clan penned up in Manurung village, with road blocks in front and behind. All their magic whatnots and paraphernalia — those long carved sticks they use. Got them all scared out of their minds! Heathen, are they still?"

Nommensen nodded. "We've a new missionary based in Laguboti now, young Steinsiek you remember. He's visited both villages with one of the Batak pendetas. But they've been very resistant to the gospel so far."

"Well," said the Dutch officer, "we've tried to do it their way. Sent some of the rajas in from Laguboti as mediators. Paid them for it, of course. But it did no good. Neither side wanted peace. They're all looking after their own interests. All the same, the lot of them! So I've come to inform you, Bishop Nommensen, that I'll have to send the troops in."

"What do you mean?"

"I'm going to send the army in to put an end to it."

Nommensen sat in silence, his head bowed.

The last few years had seen a tremendous expansion of the gospel. From his new home in Sigumpar he could look round the southern shore of Lake Toba and see village after village where churches had been built and congregations established. The presence of the Dutch East India Company undoubtedly helped bring order and stability into the region. Dutch officers had always expressed willingness to send in a vanguard of troops if any problem should arise. But Nommensen had always refused, as far as possible, preferring to trust in Christ, the most powerful Vanguard.

"There's no other way." The Controller's sharp voice cut across Nommensen's thoughts. "The Hasibuan are besieging Manurung. Shots have already been fired. Stones have been thrown. The only way to quell this thing now is by force."

Van Dijk settled back in his chair with an air of finality.

"I oppose all use of force, Mr van Dijk," said the bishop. "I'd like to ask you, if you would, to leave this affair in my hands. I can send one of my ministers there, a man who's been used before to make peace between warring villages. I rather think there's a family connection we can make use of too. He's a Lumbantobing, and the Tobings are a sub-clan of the Hasibuan."

"Ye-es." Van Dijk nodded doubtfully. "Well — I don't hold out much hope, Bishop. We tried the rajas before, you know. But I promise I'll wait and see the results of your efforts before we take any further action."

He stood up with a brisk nod to take his leave. Nommensen sat for a while gazing out across the calm water before sending a messenger to Lumban Bagasan Toba.

Cleopas was gaining a reputation as a peacemaker. Batak adat provided innumerable means of resolving conflicts through an intermediary. However much he opposed the old gods, Cleopas was adept at utilizing tradition to further the gospel of peace. Through the Batak marga or clan system he was part of the intricate tracery of a family tree whose roots and shoots permeated the whole of society. Each Batak had an established place. He owed honour to his hulahula (literally "father-in-law"), which included all his wife's or his mother's extended family, and he received honour from his boru (literally "daughter"), which extended to all his sons-in-law's families. The Hasibuan marga traditionally gave their daughters in marriage to the Manurung, creating a feudal-like relationship of protection from the Hasibuan side, and honour and service from the Manurung. But instead of protecting their boru, the Hasibuan seemed determined to wipe them out.

Cleopas went with an assistant to Manurung village near Laguboti. He found the raja of Hasibuan on the open ground in front of the village. He was surrounded by his strongest soldiers, who were milling around loading rifles, piling up rocks, yelling threats at the enemy and generally preparing themselves for battle. Cleopas slipped off his ulos as he approached, and waved the shawl aloft.

"We're friends! We come to bring you good news!"

The raja stood waiting.

"Horas, honoured raja!" called out Cleopas. "And horas to you too, Ompu," he added with a bow to the raja's chief counsellor. "We share the same ancestors. I'm a son of Raja Ginjang. So stop your warfare, please, because I've brought you important news of great benefit to you and all your people."

The raja welcomed the minister with all due ceremony and

gestured for him to sit down on the battlefield. Cleopas shook his head.

"Ompu, hear my request first. It's better that we should talk in your village. Stop this fighting for now and send everyone home. If you're not satisfied with the results of our conversation, then you can come back later and continue the war."

The raja looked from Cleopas to his counsellor, and across to the enemy village. He stood in awe of Ginjang and did not want to refuse the request out of hand. But he had expended a great deal of time, men and money in this conflict already, and now it might all be wasted.

"My two dear friends," he said in a voice of concern. "You must surely be tired from your journey. Let me send someone to escort you to our own village to rest. You can wait for us there. Our business here will soon be finished, and then we can talk as much as you like. As for peace ..." he shrugged. "We've spent a lot of money already on the rajas the Dutch Company sent, who were supposed to be working for reconciliation. But nothing was achieved — in fact it only added to our losses!" He took their arms in an expansive gesture. "So rest first in our village, both of you. The women can look after you while you wait."

Cleopas stood his ground. "It's forbidden in Batak adat for you to refuse the request of a raja — especially a raja from the same marga. We haven't come seeking a reward. In fact, we want to give you a reward!" He tossed his head. "So don't regret it later if Silindung supports Manurung. Because you'd surely be defeated then!"

The raja stared at Cleopas. It was true that a raja should be treated with honour.

"Besides which, is it justified in our adat to make war on our boru? Surely we have a duty to protect them?"

With a grunt the raja turned to his datu and told him to pull up the pangulabalang staffs guarding the two entrances to the enemy village. Cleopas called up to the raja of Manurung, who was watching in amazement from the top of the wall, that he must bring his leading men to a peace-meeting. Soon the leaders of both clans were seated sullenly on rattan mats in the sopo of Hasibuan village. Cleopas spoke first.

"I have come here, honoured rajas, not only because Bishop Nommensen sent me at the request of the Company, not only because my father Ompu Ginjang sent me, but because I myself am one family with you. The Hasibuan are our ancestors and the Manurung are our boru. I feel ashamed," he said, voicing the worst emotion that a Batak can feel. "Ashamed to think that we can't settle our differences according to adat."

He reminded them again of the warm relationship which should exist between the hulahula and the boru. Surely the hulahula should "do much without being weary", according to the old proverb, and the boru should honour and obey the hulahula as bride-giver. To fight each other, as they were doing, brought shame on them all in the eyes of Batak society.

By the time he finished, there were murmurs of agreement from all sides. The raja of Hasibuan rose to make his speech.

"Thank you, Pendeta Cleopas," he said. "We do believe that you've come out of love for your marga and your boru, and we'll do whatever you think best."

As a sign of peace the Manurung gave a piso, the traditional gift from the boru to the hulahula, in the form of some gold and a waterbuffalo, to be killed at once and eaten at the peace feast. The Hasibuan gave an ulos, the traditional Batak shawl, together with a waterbuffalo which the boru could take home. Both sides professed themselves well satisfied.

"And they want to know more about the gospel," reported Cleopas. "They would never listen before. But if Pendeta Steinsiek is still willing, they'd like him to give catechism classes in both villages."

"Wonderful! I'll tell him." Bishop Nommensen beamed his pleasure. "It's as we work like this, to reconcile Batak with Batak, that we give them a picture of what God is like: the God of love, who reconciled us to himself through Christ and gave us the ministry of reconciliation."

He glanced down at the letter he had been reading when Cleopas arrived. "But I want you to help me now with a more difficult work of reconciliation. Here."

The minister took the letter, his eyes widening as he noted the impressive seal with its twelve points and closely inscribed legend in both Batak and Arabic script.

"I've been corresponding for a while now with Raja Sisingamangaraja," said Nommensen. "I've been trying to persuade him that we are here to serve the gospel of Christ, not as agents for the Dutch. But I also wrote to him that I believe his people would benefit if he made peace with the Dutch. And I've offered to act as mediator."

"Between Sisingamangaraja and the Dutch East India Company?" Cleopas looked doubtful.

The bishop nodded. "Not easy, I know. He's the leader of Batak resistance, and he hates the Dutch. But can he really drive them out? The last attempt only brought violence and destruction, and his own people suffered. God's Church too! I've asked the raja to meet me, so that at least we can talk face to face about these things. I hope he believes that I love the Batak people too, and my only desire is for peace."

"And this is his reply?"

"That's the reply. He's agreed to meet me, and he names a date and a place."

"Lintongnihuta." Cleopas read out the name. "But that's deep in the forest, Ompu!"

"And he wants to meet about three weeks from now. You'll come with me?"

Cleopas nodded thoughtfully. "We'll need a few days for the journey."

They went by boat from Sigumpar round the southern end of Lake Toba to a point at the edge of Sisingamangaraja's territory.

From there Nommensen sent a messenger to Bakara, the raja's headquarters, as a gesture of respect to tell the raja that the bishop was already on his way to the meeting place. The main party, Nommensen, Cleopas and two helpers, set off up the mountainside, passing by ricefields on the lower, gentler slopes, and then climbing steeply up through thick forest. They rested overnight at a high point overlooking the lake.

Cleopas stood on the ridge as the sun rose next morning, watching the clouds drift across the water, shrouding Samosir Island in a white mist, and then lifting to reveal a grey-green expanse of flat-topped mountain wall. The main part of the lake stretched out into the distance, to regions as yet unknown. But to the right he could see the deep bay where Lake Toba kicked out a foot and sent off a stream of water into the Asahan River. On the distant shore was Lumban Bagasan Toba. It was too far to make out the village under its green camouflage of bamboo, but there was a tiny pale shape which might be the church.

"Beautiful, isn't it!" The bishop's soft voice broke in on his thoughts. "I can remember years ago looking down on that deep blue water with the green mountains towering up all round, and the stately pine trees. And in my mind I saw a picture of hundreds of churches dotted around the lake, and heard a ringing in my ears of church bells and the rich music of Batak voices singing praise to God for His wonderful creation."

They stood in silence, drinking in the scene. The pine-clad mountain ridges reaching down on their left to the shimmering lake water below; the straggling buildings of Laguboti round to the right; and the open plain beyond, glowing green and gold with clumps of a darker green marking the villages, and churches scattered here and there between.

"Hundreds of churches," murmured Cleopas.

"And the mountains ringing with God's praises. It's beginning. Yes, it's beginning to come true. But we've a long way to go yet. Look!" He swung Cleopas round to face the other way. "That village down there, that's where Bonn's house burnt down. And Bakara is over there to the west, the home of Sisingamangaraja. No churches yet in all that region. But if the raja will talk with me ... if I can share the gospel a little ..."

He sighed, and gave Cleopas a gentle pat on the shoulder. "Come on. We've a hard trek ahead of us yet."

The next stage of their journey was much more difficult. They hacked their way step by step through rarely traversed woodland, or moved cautiously forward along narrow, slippery paths which clung to the sides of deep ravines. Grasping at roots and undergrowth sticking out from the cliff at one side, and conscious of the ground plunging down beneath his feet on the other, Nommensen was reminded of his earliest travels in Sumatra. But he was older now — though strong and healthy for his 56 years — and more used to riding on horseback along well-beaten roads. He was glad of Cleopas, waiting patiently to guide his steps or to give him a hand across the more dangerous stretches.

They were tired and sweaty and very relieved when they emerged into an open area and saw ahead of them the ricefields of Lintongnihuta. As they drew near, the bishop's messenger came to meet them.

"Heman!" called Nommensen, surprised. "You've done well to get here so quickly. Is Ompu Sisingamangaraja here already?"

The messenger's face was solemn. "All our efforts have been wasted!"

"What's happened? What's the matter?"

"He won't meet you. He wants you to go back to Sigumpar."

Nommensen sat down heavily on a convenient tree trunk, and motioned to the others to do likewise. "But why?" He had been sure that Sisingamangaraja would keep his promise.

Heman kicked moodily at a pebble as he told his story.

"At first Ompu Sisingamangaraja was very pleased to hear that you were coming. But then they had a council meeting, with all his advisers. And the chief adviser, his datu, said that there was no way you could possibly make peace between the raja and the Dutch Company, so it was no use the raja coming to meet you."

"And did he give a reason?"

"He said that the Dutch have already spent a great amount of time and money in an effort to capture Raja Sisingamangaraja. He said that the Dutch have one aim and one aim only, which is to kill Sisingamangaraja."

Nommensen and Cleopas were silent, their faces expressionless.

"And the datu also said," continued Heman, scraping away at the loose soil with his heel. "He said that they would do well to be suspicious of your coming here. He's a very powerful man, I think, and the raja listens to him. So when he said he was suspicious of you, Ompu, then all the others started nodding their heads and frowning, and warning the raja to take care. The datu said it might be a trap. The bishop might somehow have brought along a troop of Dutch soldiers, secretly, to arrest the raja."

"A troop of soldiers!" scoffed Cleopas. "Along the way we came! It may be a better route from Bakara, but from our end you couldn't possibly do it secretly."

Nommensen shook his head sadly.

"So no one came?" asked Cleopas. "He didn't even send one of his men, as a messenger?"

Heman shook his head.

"They didn't trust us," said Nommensen. "That's all there is to it. It's very disappointing."

"So what do we do now?"

"We go home, my friends, we go home. There's nothing else we can do." Nommensen grimaced at the thought of the slippery footpaths, then laughed. "I warned you this would be a difficult one! But we've done what we can, and seen some beautiful scenery on the way. So let's sing as we go, and leave the outcome in the Lord's hands."

11 BUILDING BRIDGES

One morning in 1894 Cleopas met Pendeta Steinsiek, the missionary from Laguboti, walking slowly along the road with an abstracted frown on his face.

"Good morning, Ompu."

"Oh! Good morning, Cleopas." The missionary looked up with a start. "I was just coming to see you, actually."

"Are you worried about something?" asked Cleopas as they turned onto the path to Lumban Bagasan.

"Ye-es. Mmm. Not exactly. I've been teaching a catechism class, and then I thought I'd call and see how you all are."

"We're doing fine, Ompu."

"And your wife?"

Cleopas nodded. After four sons, Petronella had given birth in March to twin girls, Margaret and Deborah. But after only three months Deborah had died.

"She's been very upset, of course," said Cleopas. "We all have. But the little one was always weak, you know. It's very unusual here for both twins to live."

"I've noticed." A mother would often feed the stronger baby first to be sure that one, at least, survived. But the missionary did not mention this.

"It's considered a great misfortune in Batak adat to have twins," said Cleopas. "In the old days one baby was destroyed at birth, just as I myself was nearly killed. The old spirits were very harsh." He smiled sadly. "We received them both, of course, as a gift from

God, but it seems that the one was more of a loan."

Petronella was resting with her baby, but she soon bustled about making coffee for the visitor. She had been very much helped, she told him with a smile, by all the church families, and she thanked God daily for His loving care.

"But I think you were worried about something, Pendeta Steinsiek," said Cleopas.

"Ye-es. I saw something rather odd this morning, very early, when I was going off to take my catechism class. It looked like a fire burning, a little way off the road, and when I went to see, there was a hut on fire. Poor sort of place, but it might have been someone's home. And a whole crowd of people gathered round." He frowned. "That's why I didn't stop then. There seemed plenty of people to help, and I'd promised to go early to the village, before folks started work in the fields. Only ..."

"Only?"

Steinsiek shrugged his shoulders. "Only I have this strange feeling that they weren't trying to put the fire out at all! Quite the opposite, in fact."

Cleopas and his wife exchanged glances.

"So I was wondering if you'd come back there with me now, Cleopas, and help me to find out what was going on?"

"Yes, I'll come," said Cleopas. "I have an idea what it might be. Don't worry," he added, in answer to a frown from Petronella. "I won't touch anything."

They found the place quite easily: it was a small clearing at the edge of the forest, some way back from the main road. The crowd had gone, but a man stood guard over the fire which was nibbling away fretfully at the burnt-out frame of the hut. As they approached he poked at the smouldering embers with a stick so that they sparked into life.

"Hey!" called Steinsiek, darting forward. "What's been going on here? What was happening this morning? And what are you doing there, keeping the fire going instead of working to put it out?"

"A woman with leprosy lived here," said the man, with another poke at the fire. "And this morning her hut was burned down, together with the woman."

"And where is the woman now?" asked Steinsiek.

The man looked from missionary to minister and back.

"Over there," he said, pointing with his stick to a charred heap on the ground.

Steinsiek stood in silence, looking down at the body. She had been a young woman, one of a small group who came to beg sometimes by the roadside.

"You couldn't have saved her," said Cleopas, as they walked home together later. "It was too late, I'm sure, by the time you went by. They would have come in the middle of the night to set fire to the place."

"You mean that was deliberate?" Steinsiek was appalled.

Cleopas nodded. "People are frightened of leprosy," he explained. "Frightened of infection. I've learned a little about it myself, from our lessons with the bishop. But there's a deep-rooted fear of leprosy in all Bataks. We think of it as a curse — a disgrace — something that brings shame not just on the sufferer but on the whole family."

"So anyone with leprosy is turned out."

"Yes. They're turned out of their homes, and they end up like that poor woman, living in dilapidated little shacks at the edge of the forest, where no one will be horrified or fearful at the sight of them."

"And how do they live?"

"That's the cruelty of it. Their families bring food at first. They leave it a short distance from the shack, so they won't have to come into direct contact with the sick person. But after a time they're too frightened or ashamed. Or they simply lose interest. They hardly think of these people as family any more. And in the end they stop coming altogether. But the leprosy sufferers still have to live! So they'll come out in gangs and terrify passersby, or they'll come out to the fields at harvest time and beg for rice. And the farmer is so scared that he'll give them what they want just to be rid of them!"

"Out of horror, not pity."

"That's right. But, of course, the wealthy don't suffer like that. If a raja gets leprosy he'll be cared for at home, and people pretend not to notice. They keep their distance though!"

"But what about that hut burning down?" asked Steinsiek. "If the sick are sent off away somewhere, do they have to be murdered too?"

Cleopas took the missionary's arm. "That is the power of the datu," he said solemnly. "Something happens: a cholera epidemic, or a harvest failure, or they lose in war with an enemy marga. So the villagers ask, 'Why didn't the spirits protect us?' And the datu says, 'The ancestors won't come near you because of those ugly people with leprosy.' So, in the middle of the night when they are sure the sick person will be asleep, two or three men will creep out of the village and set fire to the shelter."

"So the patient burns to death!"

Cleopas nodded. "Then they feel the curse of leprosy has been completely wiped out."

"We must do something!" said Steinsiek. "Find someone who can help these poor people. And teach the Christians they must have compassion for those who suffer, not hate and fear!"

"At home we pray for those with leprosy in our family prayers," said Cleopas. "I've preached on the need to show practical love to these people, and I've talked sometimes with the rajas about it. But I've met with a very cold response so far."

"Don't give up," said Steinsiek. "Let's keep on praying for them. And we'll talk with the bishop. See if he can see a way of helping them."

Two German deaconesses were based in Laguboti now, running a children's home and teaching the women and girls in the church. They began to make regular visits to the homes of the leprosy sufferers, and Steinsiek arranged for the patients to receive a weekly allowance of rice and salt.

Then Steinsiek wrote to Cleopas that an army doctor had expressed interest in the problems of leprosy and would like Cleopas to accompany him and Sister Nieman on a visit to those patients living around Laguboti.

They went first to see a young man who had narrowly escaped death when his hut had been burned down by angry Bataks. He backed away in fright when the visitors appeared suddenly at the door of his new shelter. But Sister Nieman's soothing voice, reminding him of visits she had made in the past and explaining that here was a doctor with medicine to help his sickness, drew him slowly forward. Then the doctor was able to take him gently by the arm and lead him out into the light.

Cleopas watched in awe as the doctor and nurse examined the sick man, touching and prodding his disease-ridden limbs with no sign of shrinking or fear of infection. Gradually the pendeta was able to overcome his own guilty feelings of revulsion enough to give help as needed, pouring out medicine and preparing the food they had brought.

"It's not contagious," said the doctor. "There's really no need to isolate anyone with leprosy. But people see the deformities and are repelled or frightened. So besides the physical suffering the patients have to suffer emotionally: thrown out by their own families, insulted, starved to death or burnt out of their homes like this young man. What they suffer is beyond belief!"

He patted the man's arm. "Sister Nieman will come to see you once a week," he said in a slow, deliberate voice. "You must do what she tells you." Cleopas repeated his words to make sure the man understood.

The patient gave an awkward smile. He stood watching from his doorway as they went down the track to the next little shack.

"No one has yet discovered an exact cure for leprosy," the

doctor explained as they walked on. "But we live in hopes. And you must pray, Pendeta, for God's blessing on the medicine we give, so that God will work to bring healing."

Cleopas visited the leprosy patients often after this, sometimes with the doctor or Sister Nieman, but sometimes on his own, just to talk and to share the gospel with them. Most lived in a constant state of anxiety, and Cleopas began to wonder if some sort of settlement might be built where they could live together in safety and receive regular treatment.

"I've been thinking about that too," said the doctor when Cleopas broached the subject with him. "But talk to them first about it. Best to find out if they would be prepared to move, before we start preparing a place for them."

Most of the patients were bewildered by this suggestion at first. They had so little contact with other people, and their experiences had convinced them that no one cared. They found it difficult to grasp the minister's suggestion, and when they did understand they suspected his motives. This must surely be a plot hatched by "that Dutchman" to herd them together and then kill them all at once. But gradually, as Cleopas continued to visit and to explain his idea, they became more receptive.

Bishop Nommensen gave his ready approval for the project, and Steinsiek and Cleopas spent many hours visiting the rajas of the district to gain their support and cooperation. Eventually the rajas agreed to give a large piece of land near Sigumpar, where Nommensen lived. A settlement of simple houses was erected, called Hutasalem: "Peacetown".

Cleopas was given the task of rounding up the leprosy sufferers and bringing them to Hutasalem. Most came happily, but a few were wary still, and held back till they saw how well their fellows were faring. The doctor and nurse visited the settlement once a week to examine the patients and give out medicine, and a church elder was made responsible for the day-to-day care. Cleopas visited regularly too, to pray with the patients and share the gospel.

Soon he was holding catechism classes, and a number came to trust in Christ.

Cleopas and his family were moving house at that time, back to Silindung valley. After a total of twelve years by Lake Toba, two as evangelist and ten as minister, Cleopas was appointed to the church at Sipoholon in September 1899.

The Aek Sigaeon River, flowing through Silindung valley, cut the parish of Sipoholon in two. In the dry season the river could be forded, but in the wet season the current was swift and the water deep, so that villages on the far side were quite isolated. Culliman, the missionary responsible for the district, had found it impossible to visit his church members, and in his frustration had suggested to the local rajas that they should build a bridge, or preferably two bridges, across the river. The rajas had agreed to this, but over a year later nothing had been done on the project.

"I'm hoping you can mobilize these Bataks," Culliman said to Cleopas as he welcomed the family to Sipoholon. "The whole valley would benefit if we had a bridge across the river here. The bishop tells me that you've done some good work in the past in getting churches and schools built."

"A little," said Cleopas. "I can ask the rajas about it when we visit them."

By tradition, newcomers to a district must always visit their neighbours to introduce themselves. This was even more important when it was a case of the new minister visiting his flock. Cleopas and Petronella went to see all the rajas and leading men of the district, and they used the opportunity to ask why the building work had been held up. Usually the answer was the same.

"Let him build the bridge himself if he wants one that badly. We don't like being treated like coolies."

"That missionary doesn't want to listen to our opinions; he thinks he's the one with all the power and authority. Well, if he's so powerful, let him build the bridges himself!"

In some trepidation Cleopas went to see Culliman, and explained to him as tactfully as he could the nature of the problem. Culliman was astounded.

"But I'd no idea they felt like that! They all smiled and nodded and agreed with me that a bridge would be a very good thing. I thought they were all set to go ahead and build it!"

"We Bataks are a very proud people," said Cleopas. "And so many of our traditions are to do with status and respect. A raja must always be treated with honour. We speak gently, submissively to our superiors, and call them Ompu, Grandfather, even if they're still quite young. And we shout our commands to those beneath us. But the Company men come along and stand with their hands on their hips to show they're the boss, and order everyone around, great or small."

"Oh, but ..."

"I know the missionaries are different, Mr Culliman. Ompu Nommensen has been like a father to me... more than a father. I know you come here because you love God and want to serve Him, and to love and care for us. But many of the rajas don't know that yet. They hear your voice and think you're demanding, not suggesting, and they quickly take offence." He grinned ruefully. "That's another thing you must surely have noticed about the Bataks. We can flare up in an instant! That's why we have so many wars."

"Well, we don't want a war on our hands," laughed Culliman. "Thank you for being so open with me, Cleopas. I think I'd better leave it to you now. Let's see if we can find a way to start again with a clean sheet. I'll be happy to make my apologies to these rajas."

Cleopas invited all the rajas to a meeting at the church in Sipoholon. Culliman came too, and he began by expressing his personal regret that the building work had been neglected. One of the older rajas acted as spokesman for the rest.

"I'll speak frankly," he said, "as you've asked us to tell you the reason. We know that the whole point of these bridges is to benefit us, so that we can cross the river and visit our friends and relatives on the far side. But we don't like Mr Culliman treating us like coolies."

Culliman said nothing.

"We all feel the same," said another Batak. "He acts like he's the big boss and we're all just dirt under his feet."

"Yes, that's true!"

The grumbles were hushed as the missionary got to his feet.

"Honoured rajas," he said, "I want to ask your forgiveness for all the faults I've shown as I've ministered here over the past two years. I'm a foreigner here, and even though I worked in Sibolga for some years, I know that I still have much to learn about the way Bataks do things. Please believe me that I had no intention of offending you in any way. I do regret the mistakes I've made. In fact I came here today especially to apologize."

As they listened to this open speech, the hard, angry faces of the Batak rajas softened into warmth and amazement. Apologies are never easy, but for a westerner to ask forgiveness of Bataks was revolutionary! Cold resentment sparked into enthusiasm. Everyone was ready with suggestions as to how the bridges might best be built.

"Let's have one bridge upstream, next to my village. I can get my men working on it in no time."

"We can help you by bringing the timber."

"And I can get my men working from the other side."

"Good." The earlier spokesman stood up. "So the raja of Simanungkalit will be responsible for the bridge upstream, with the help of you two rajas. Agreed?"

They nodded.

"And we'll build the second bridge downstream, by my village, and those of us who live nearby will bring our people to work on it. Right?"

"Thank you very much, Ompu," said Cleopas.

"But we have one condition, Pendeta."

"And that is?"

"No interference. We'll do the job. Mr Culliman and yourself, Pendeta Cleopas, you don't need to do anything now. We'll do it better without any interference."

"Yes, Ompu, we'll happily agree to that," said Cleopas with a smile.

Three weeks later the two bridges were ready for use.

12 SERPENTS AND DOVES

The seminary site at Pansur Napitu was very cramped. Early in 1900, at the three-monthly ministers' meeting, it was decided to move it to Sipoholon. Culliman and Cleopas were given the task of finding a suitable site. Cleopas had heard of a place across the river, a field which the Dutch army had earlier used for target practice.

"There's only one problem," he said, as they walked up the track from the newly built bridge. "But it may be a big one."

The site was some distance from the river by a little village called Lumban Rang. It had a wide expanse of gently sloping land backed by steep pine-clad hills.

"Beautiful," said Culliman, breathing in the fresh, pine-scented air. "But it would be difficult to bring water all that way up from the river. Impossible, even."

"There's a large source of water right behind those hills," said Cleopas. "Not very far away, actually, if only there were a way through."

"Could we cut a channel, do you think?" Culliman pulled at his moustache. "Wouldn't be easy. Not easy at all. Maybe we should go round — or over? Take a look at the other side before we decide anything."

A few days later Cleopas called a meeting of all the rajas and told them of the plan to move the seminary to Sipoholon.

"This would be of great benefit to the people of Sipoholon," he said. "Maybe your own sons can be educated there! But there's

only one possible site. And before a seminary could be built there
we have to solve the problem of the water supply."

Everyone agreed that they wanted the seminary at Sipoholon.
But after toing and froing and examining every possible side of
the water question, it seemed the only possibility was to cut through
the range of hills. It was a daunting prospect.

"I'd like to suggest, honoured rajas, that first we try to clear
the ground," said Cleopas. "Then we can examine the whole area
very closely, and see if we can work out the best way to proceed."

"We can only say that we're ready to help," said the raja of
Simanungkalit. "We'll organize our people to clear the ground for
you, and if you decide to go ahead with the project, we'll help
in whatever way we can."

The Bataks turned out in large numbers. Some chopped down
trees, others carried off the timber or cleared away the thick
tangle of undergrowth. In a matter of days a broad band of
cleared land lay open to view. Cleopas walked slowly over the
hilltop with two of the rajas, examining the ground to plot out
more precisely the route they should cut. Then another meeting
was called.

"It's a difficult task, and perhaps a dangerous one," he acknowledged. "Do you feel you can go ahead?"

"Yes, Pendeta. We'll try."

After a lengthy discussion, the various tasks were assigned, and
they agreed to start work immediately.

The rajas were enthusiastic. One team would dig while
another team cleared away, and others brought water to soften
the earth. Cleopas was constantly on site, encouraging, supervising,
making suggestions. Remembering the problems over the bridge,
he was very careful to consult with the rajas before making a decision, so that at every stage of the work he had their full support.

Skilled workers were brought in from outside the district. Their
knowledge and experience would guide the more difficult aspects
of the work, such as determining how steep the the slope should

be. Otherwise landslides might occur in the heavy rain. Even with this care, an accident happened.

The channel was deep. Three men were digging together near the top of the slope when one put a foot wrong and started a landslide. Earth and rocks hurtled down the steep side of the channel, raising thick clouds of dust and carrying all three down with them. Choking and blinded, they grabbed at the earth as they fell. Two managed to grasp at roots but then were buried under the avalanche. The third fell right to the bottom.

Everyone rushed up as they heard the muffled screams and the rush of falling earth.

"Where are they? What's happened?"

"Look there!"

At the bottom of the channel a mound of earth parted, and a man's hand could be seen. Then his head emerged as he struggled to escape.

"Get a rope. Quick!"

Two workers were lowered into the pit to help the wounded man, still dazed and breathless. Carefully they lifted him up to the surface.

"My friends! Where are they?"

"There are more?"

Frantically the search party began scrabbling through the rubble. Cleopas arrived as they uncovered the missing men. Both were dead.

Messengers went off to tell their families. All work stopped as the two bodies were carried back to their homes. The funeral was held that afternoon.

Next day the work continued, but the spirit was gone. No one would work near the spot where the men had been killed. Cleopas was forced to look for new workers to dig that stretch of the channel, and they demanded higher wages. Many refused to come back to work altogether.

Cleopas visited the rajas with Luke the Bible teacher and two church elders.

"We'd better give up," said one raja. "God is no longer pro-tecting us, so we must stop before anything worse happens."

"That land was sacred to the spirits once, where you're trying to build a seminary. It's quite clear that our ancestors don't want you there. They'll stop you building."

"I'm sure that God will help us if we trust Him," urged Cleopas.

"Could you not try once more?" added Luke.

But it was no good. The rajas who had been frightened by the incident could not be persuaded. Cleopas decided to continue with-out them. And gradually, over a period of two or three weeks, people began to drift back to work.

There were more frightening incidents, times when work stopped for a moment and Cleopas led all the workers in prayer for God's protection. He would also offer thanksgiving when a difficult or dangerous section was completed without mishap. No further accidents occurred, and the aqueduct was completed near the end of 1900. The workers shouted with joy as they saw the first water swirling through the channel they had made.

At this point Cleopas handed over the project to Pendeta Culliman, who was to take charge of building the seminary. Culliman sent a messenger to Pearaja, informing the bishop that the aqueduct was completed and inviting the church leaders to come and inspect the site. A few days later Dr John Warneck, principal of the seminary at Pansur Napitu, arrived with Mr Metzler from the office at Pearaja.

Cleopas was away at that time, visiting a new congregation in a very poor area and setting up the main pillar for a church building. Passing near Culliman's house on his way home, he decided to call in to tell the missionary how the new group was developing. Mrs Culliman came to the door with a gloomy frown instead of her usual cheerful smile. Culliman himself was looking extremely tense.

"What's happened?" asked Cleopas. "Didn't the missionaries

come from Pearaja?"

"Oh yes, they came all right!" said Culliman.

Warneck and Metzler had arrived that morning and were very impressed with the new aqueduct. They had asked how much of the land was being given for the seminary. The boundaries had earlier been agreed on by all the Sipoholon rajas. So Culliman asked the raja of Simanungkalit, his assistant in the building, to indicate the boundaries with posts in the ground.

Some boys from the nearby village of Lumban Rang had come out to watch the visitors, and the raja told them to stick the posts in the ground, showing them where each should go. As the missionaries stood watching, Culliman explained his ideas for positioning the various seminary buildings.

Suddenly the raja of Lumban Rang, Ompur Sangga, stormed out of his fortified village and growled at the boys to pull up the posts immediately.

"So you think you can do what you want here, do you?" he shouted. "Coming along to a piece of land that doesn't belong to you and staking out your territory! Don't you know that this is my land? How dare you stake it out without asking my permission?"

"Ompu, I'm sorry," said Culliman. "I told him to put the posts in. We ..."

"This is my land!" yelled the raja. "Don't you know that all the land around here is under my authority as raja?"

"Yes, Ompu, but we were only marking out the boundaries we'd agreed on. I'm sorry we didn't call to see you first."

Culliman tried to calm the raja down, but he would not be calmed. Warneck and Metzler tried to mediate, but the raja took no notice.

"Don't you know," he barked, "that even when the Company came to use this land for target practice, they asked my permission first? But you come along here — you're going to break up all this ground and build houses, and have a settlement here! All without one word to let us know, or to ask permission!"

"But we'd already ..."

"What you are doing isn't law and it isn't adat! Your under-
ling there," he pointed scathingly with his chin, "who you've made
a church elder, thinks that because he's the raja of Simanungkalit
he must be raja here too!"

Hearing the accusation, Warneck turned to Culliman.

"You've made a big mistake here," he said angrily. "We thought
you'd completed all the preparations, and that was why you'd
invited us. But clearly there's a long way to go yet. And how
could you choose as your assistant for this project a man who's
on such bad terms with the local raja?"

With a brief nod to the raja, the two missionaries mounted
their horses and left. They refused to call back at Culliman's house,
even though Mrs Culliman had a meal waiting for them.

"Of course, none of this would have happened, I don't sup-
pose," said Culliman, "if I'd taken them first to be introduced to
Raja Sangga."

"Or if the elder hadn't asked Sangga's boys to stick the posts
in," suggested his wife.

Cleopas had listened in amazement. He tried to comfort the
missionary, who was clearly feeling utterly depressed.

"You couldn't know what would happen," said Cleopas. "But
don't worry. We can sort it all out with some good Batak nego-
tiating. Tomorrow morning we'll go together to visit Ompu Sangga.
But you'd better bring along plenty of money. Say two hundred
silver dollars. And I'll ask my Bible teacher, Luke, to come too,
because he's a son of Raja Pontas. We'll invite Ompu Augustine
as well. He's really the high raja of all the Sipoholon villages, so
Raja Sangga should respect his authority."

"If I'd known all this trouble would arise, I'd never have let
you go off on that trip," said Culliman, feeling relieved already.
"I'll let you take the lead, Cleopas, and let's hope we can clear
it all up."

Next day Culliman, Luke, Cleopas and Ompu Augustine set off to visit Raja Sangga. The raja was deep in discussion with a group of men as they approached the village, and did not see them coming until Cleopas stood almost in front of him.

"Don't be embarrassed, honoured raja," said Cleopas, with an airy wave of his hand. "We've come to enjoy your famous hospitality. So please will you tell your wife, with our respects, that we'd be delighted if she could cook for us? And then when we've eaten we can have a talk. As it happens, there are matters we should discuss with you."

"Yes, of course, and welcome," said Raja Sangga, with a deep bow to Augustine and a nod to the rest.

He muttered a short command to a servant, and then ushered his guests across to the sopo where they could sit in state. As they waited, the conversation ranged freely over the state of their crops and the health of their families, but never once approached the subject on everyone's mind.

After a delicious meal, Cleopas opened the conversation by thanking their host for his kindness and expressing the hope that he and his family would enjoy health and prosperity.

"And what might be the purpose of your visit?" asked Raja Sangga.

"Our purpose in coming here, Ompu," replied Cleopas. "is to seek the fulfilment of a promise made to our two fathers, Ompu Ginjang and Ompu Pontas. You asked them to make peace once between this village and Simanungkalit, when the raja of Simanungkalit was all set to burn down your village."

The raja nodded. "Yes, they did mediate the peace."

"Raja Pontas, as you know, has only recently been called into the Lord's presence. But his son Luke here and myself have been entrusted with the task of receiving from you the token of that promise of friendship. In other words, Ompu, we have come with Ompu Augustine and Mr Culliman as witnesses, in the hope that you can present us with an ulos, in the traditional manner."

"Why certainly, my friends," said Sangga with a smile. "We Bataks always seal our friendships by enfolding our friends in this special Batak shawl," he explained in a gracious aside to the missionary. "Quick," he called to a servant. "bring two uloses."

"I have been waiting to perform this ceremony," he told them. "But your honoured fathers never came. So if this is your purpose, then I am happy to give you each this token so that our relationship with the rajas of Silindung will be strengthened."

Two shawls were brought out, closely woven in dark colours. The raja solemnly draped one round the shoulders of the pendeta, and the other round the teacher.

"Now, Ompu," said Cleopas, "we have received the ulos, which you have wrapped around us. So according to adat we must offer the gift which is given in return, the piso. I hope you will tell us what you would like as a piso. We had thought perhaps of giving you a saddle horse so you can ride to meetings?"

"Give seventy dollars," suggested Raja Augustine, prompt on cue. "We are better at choosing horses ourselves."

Raja Sangga agreed to this suggestion, and the pendeta counted out seventy dollars. "May the promise of friendship which has been confirmed by both sides bring blessing and prosperity to all," he said as he handed over the money.

"Just so," replied the raja. "May we be closer, and our friendship firm." After a brief pause he added, "And now that our relationship is clear, I hope that you both, Pendeta Cleopas and Teacher Luke, will feel free to make use of that old firing range. Build a village on it or a school or something. It's up to you."

"Thank you very much, Ompu," said Cleopas. "We welcome this sign of your generosity, and we trust the Lord will bless you because of it. And in the name of the church which is going to build the seminary here, Mr Culliman and I would like to thank you. But so that everything is completely clear, may I suggest that we meet tomorrow morning and stake out the boundary posts together."

Culliman breathed a sigh of relief as they stood up to make their farewells.

But at the last moment all their efforts were nearly overturned. Someone had been watching when Cleopas handed over the money, and now a very old man appeared, wearing the elaborate tunic of a raja and surrounded by an entourage of sturdy Bataks.

"Raja Sangga," he said, in a tone of great displeasure, "we all agreed that no one should sell land unless we all reached a common agreement. But now I hear that you have sold your land without telling us. Your action is against the law and against our adat."

Remembering his guests, Raja Sangga tried to answer in a calm voice. "The pendeta and the Bible teacher came here in accordance with adat. I have given them each an ulos to fulfil an earlier promise, and I received from them in return a piso in the form of money."

The old man waved away this explanation.

"That's just an excuse. It's quite clear that you have received money, and we've had no share in it. You've been honoured, and we have been neglected. If you are selling your land, then we want to sell our land too. The pendeta should give us some money for our land too."

After a whispered consultation with Culliman on one side, Cleopas asked everyone to sit down again.

"Honoured rajas," he said, "our aim is to bring peace and friendship. We don't want to have any misunderstandings. So let me explain that we came here to fulfil an obligation according to Batak adat. We have received an ulos from the raja here, and so in response it is our duty to give a piso. The money which you saw me give to Raja Sangga was instead of a saddle-horse, at the suggestion of our high raja, Ompu Augustine."

There was a disgruntled murmur, but Cleopas continued.

"Nevertheless, in order to wipe out any unworthy suspicions, as we received some land in addition to the ulos, then we are willing to buy from you the land next to Raja Sangga's."

This suggestion met with general approval, and Culliman gave the old raja and his friends a sum of money which Ompu Augustine considered a fair price for their land.

"We'll have to use it as a paddyfield," murmured the missionary to Cleopas. "It's far more than we need for the seminary buildings."

The next morning all the villagers from Lumban Rang gathered on the open land, and helped to drive in the boundary posts round the area which had been handed over to the church. Warneck and Metzler came back a few days later to see the land, and were delighted that what had seemed such a difficult problem had been resolved.

The building project started immediately, and by the middle of 1901 the lecture rooms, office, staff houses and student hostel were all complete. The seminary was moved that year from Pansur Napitu to Sipoholon, under the headship of Dr Warneck.

13 STONY GROUND

Beyond the new seminary a narrow track ran up through thick pine forest to lose itself in endless lines of dark green mountain ridges. This was Hullang, renowned for its benzoin trees whose bark produced a fragrant resin used to make incense. This incense, widely valued for use in spirit worship, fetched a high price from the middlemen who came up the river valley from the big seaports on the west coast of Sumatra. Cleopas visited in the region, but found them unresponsive to the gospel. He was surprised and dismayed when Bishop Nommensen asked him to live there.

"These people have had very little opportunity to hear the gospel," said Nommensen. "And I know, Cleopas, that you have the heart and the gifts of an evangelist."

Cleopas and Petronella exchanged glances. Cleopas was already forty-five years old. They had six children now, and enjoyed life in Sipoholon with its school and its facilities, and its ready access by road to Pearaja and their family. It would be hard to move to a primitive area where the roads were still difficult.

"The Lord commands us to go to every corner of the earth," said the bishop, "not only to those places which are already civilized. On the contrary, he wants us to gather in those who are not yet gathered in, to bring order where as yet there is no order, so that we can build His Church in places where He is not yet known. Isn't that so?"

The Lumbantobings moved to Hullang in June 1902, leaving their second son, Frederick, to lodge with a missionary family in Sipoholon.

There was only one Christian congregation in Hullang, in the village of Hutajulu. Cleopas made this his base. The half-finished church building, abandoned when the few Christians had lost interest, was soon completed, together with a house for the pendeta and a school. A newly qualified Bible teacher took charge of the school, leaving Cleopas free to concentrate on evangelism and pastoring his congregation. Numbers grew steadily. In December 1903 he baptised 203 adults with their children.

Cleopas visited the rajas of the nearby market town, asking permission to open a school there and to teach the gospel. The chief raja was enthusiastic, but others were more wary.

"What is it you want to do?" asked one with a frown.

"We're offering to teach your children to read and write, Ompu, and to learn about the Christian faith."

"Oh!" the raja shrugged expressive shoulders. "Why should we fret ourselves learning to read and write or puzzling over religion? We don't need God! We can make all we want from collecting incense in the forest." He adjusted his elaborately carved ivory armbands in affirmation of his prosperity. "We may live far from the big towns, but we have overflowing purses, you know!"

A school was started, nevertheless, and later a church.

The more isolated parts of Hullang were difficult to reach. A small group of keen Christians made tiring journeys on foot, climbing steep mountain sides or crossing swift-flowing rivers, sometimes over makeshift bridges slung precariously across deep ravines. In each place Cleopas began by opening a school, bringing in a teacher who could visit the local families and begin catechism classes.

The wealthy Bataks of Hullang saw little need for either education or religion. But there were shining exceptions, like the raja of Bonandolok in the north, who with the pendeta's help started three schools in his village and put up an imposing church building.

By 1907 there were ten adult congregations in Hullang. It was time to turn from evangelism to consolidation. That was when the bishop summoned Cleopas to Pearaja.

"We have a problem," he said. "We're experiencing something of a setback in the Pangaribuan district. A number of families have left the church, and most of them have turned to Islam. I'd like you to move to Pangaribuan, Cleopas, so that you can help the missionary who's based there, Pendeta Meisel."

Cleopas sat in silence for a moment. After five years of hard slogging he had looked forward to a more settled teaching ministry in Hullang.

"Yes, Ompu," he said at last. "We'll go."

On December 13th, 1907, the Lumbantobing family moved to Pangaribuan.

It was a much poorer area than Hullang, with barren soil which yielded meagre rice harvests. But with true Batak hospitality the Christians gave a great feast to welcome the new pendeta. Can it be true, wondered Cleopas, as he listened to the speeches, that the church is in decline? But he soon discovered that it was so.

Walking round their new district with Petronella, he saw many schools and teachers' houses standing empty. Churchyards were overgrown and the church buildings in disrepair. Sometimes the church workers had broken them up for firewood.

Pangaribuan, not far from Nommensen's early centre at Huta Dame, had been one of the first districts to accept Christianity. But on Sunday very few people came to the church service. When Cleopas asked about catechism classes, or women's meetings, or Bible classes for the men, he was told that they had been discontinued. From all sides could be heard the sound of the mosque drum summoning people to prayer.

"Is that where they are all going then?" he asked the Bible teacher.

"Some of them. There are three groups of people now in Pangaribuan: the Christians, the Muslims, and the ones who still worship the spirits. They're the biggest group. But we all join together when there's a funeral or a baby born, and we're having a feast." He paused. "That's what's caused all the trouble."

"The trouble?"

"Yes. Mm." The young man picked up a pebble and hurled it at a mangy dog which was snuffling round the church door. "The missionary gets angry when there's a big Batak feast, because everything gets mixed up together. You know what the adat ceremonies are like — the datu doing his dance with the magic staff and asking the ancestors to bless the harvest or whatever. These are spirit worshippers, you understand, Pendeta, not Christians."

Cleopas nodded. "Yes, I realize that."

"And then there'll be special rice offered to the ancestors, and of course we all have to eat some of it. And then the missionary gets angry with the Christians for joining in. But how could we not join in?"

"Mmm."

"So then the rajas get angry too, and stop their people coming to church."

Cleopas walked home deep in thought. What should he do? After much prayer for wisdom, he visited each congregation in turn and talked with every raja, trying as tactfully as possible to find out what had gone wrong.

When he was sure of his facts, Cleopas went to see the missionary. Bluntly he told him that the rajas were offended by his attitude to the Muslims and the spirit worshippers.

"You told them that Christians shouldn't attend the adat ceremonies. They feel very bitter about it, and that's why they won't let their people come to church or send their children to school any more."

Meisel ran his hands through his hair. "But Cleopas, how can we let Christians go offering sacrifices to the spirits? It's syncretistic! It's against Scripture! They need to learn that they can't serve two masters."

"Yes, I know we must follow one God. Accepting Christ means

that we don't follow the old ways. So of course Christians can't hold a feast to honour the spirits." He paused, wondering what to say next. "But when we preach the gospel to Bataks, we must understand Batak customs. We see things in a different way here from in the West."

"Yes," Meisel sighed. "Yes, I know. You tell me then."

"We Bataks think more in terms of community than you do," said Cleopas. "So if someone in our marga, our clan, is holding a feast, then we feel we must go to it, as part of the family. Not to go would be terribly rude."

"But if it means compromising your faith?"

"Yes I know," admitted Cleopas. "That's the problem. I've been praying and praying about it, and I don't see an easy way out. Maybe in the speeches. You know we always make speeches at feast time. Maybe then we could explain that as Christians we believe something different now. Use it as an opportunity to share the gospel."

"Ye-es," said Meisel. "Someone with a strong faith could do that."

"That's what I do, if I'm invited anywhere."

"But I'm afraid that a younger Christian would just be confused. You can't follow Jesus *and* the spirits. That's what I told them." He sighed again. "And so now it seems they don't want to follow Jesus!"

"I think, Mr Meisel," suggested Cleopas, "you are forgetting how much the Batak view of the world centres on the raja. You maybe think that we have too many rajas."

Meisel nodded fervently and Cleopas laughed.

"But there's a special aura about the raja, a sort of power or authority which everyone recognizes. The church has spread very rapidly in Batakland just because so many rajas wanted to become Christians. But if you make an enemy of the raja, then you have made enemies of the people too, and sooner or later you must pack your bags and leave."

Meisel stared at the ground for a long time. Cleopas wondered if he had been too outspoken. But eventually the missionary looked up, and clasped his hand firmly. "Yes, Cleopas," he said. "I know we both want to serve the Lord in the best possible way. Let's see if we can find a way through this one, shall we?"

In March 1908 Cleopas called a special meeting for the rajas of the district to talk with the missionary in the church at Pangaribuan. The pendeta opened the discussion.

"Honoured rajas, we have called this meeting so that as Christians who have been baptized in the name of the Father, Son and Holy Spirit, and as rajas according to Batak tradition, we can put an end to all the grumblings and resentments which are troubling our peace and brotherhood."

He told them how sad he felt to see the churches neglected, and reminded them that they themselves owned the church buildings; the ministers were only stewards on their behalf. "You yourselves are the losers if they are left to rot."

A number of rajas spoke, insisting that they were still Christians, but that they were not valued by the Church and so had not bothered to attend the services.

"We can't accept Pendeta Meisel's attitude," complained one raja. "He forbids us to play our proper part as leaders of society and to show respect to our brothers, sisters or cousins who are Muslims or who worship the spirits."

"Being Christians shouldn't mean we have to cut ourselves off and act like foreigners. Shouldn't it make us even more loving towards the people around us?"

Meisel listened in silence. When invited to speak, he apologized for not fully understanding Batak customs.

"As a foreigner coming into the midst of the Batak people", he said, "I want to become your brother and to learn how you see right and wrong. So please forgive my mistakes. In future if I do something wrong then please, as my brothers in Christ, feel free to tell me."

As had happened at Sipoholon, the rajas of Pangaribuan were totally disarmed by this open apology from a western missionary. Cleopas closed the meeting with a hymn and a prayer, and Pendeta Meisel shook hands with everyone.

After this the whole atmosphere changed. The children and the teachers came back to school, while their parents set to work clearing the churchyards and repairing church buildings. The chief raja of Pangaribuan sent for Cleopas and asked him to take charge of the church building project in his village, which had been abandoned for almost a year.

"Don't worry about materials and building costs," he added. "I shall see to that myself as an offering to redeem my sin, because I neglected the Lord's house for so long."

The problem of opposition from the Muslim leaders still remained. Many Christians had begun to study Islam during the time of conflict. But now most of them had come back to church. The Muslim leaders were annoyed about this, and told their erst-while converts that if they left Islam they would be cursed. Threats were met with counter-threats, and soon fights were breaking out all over town.

The chief raja summoned the leaders of both sides.

"If these people no longer want to recite the Muslim creed, they must not be compelled," he told the imams. "The same applies to Christianity. When they left the church and turned to Islam, the ministers didn't use force against them and certainly didn't curse them. If this trouble continues, I shall have to close the Muslim school."

Not long after this two Bataks who had been attending the mosque failed to appear at the time of prayer. They had gone with friends to a church service in another village. When they came home they found their Muslim neighbours waiting. Insults were exchanged and then blows, and in an instant the whole village was in an uproar.

The raja was furious. He marched out in a rage and ordered

the Muslim school to be pulled down and the imams to leave the district the next day.

This prompt action did little to cool the tensions.

At about that time, at a meeting of church members, all the rajas in the district decided that the Ten Commandments should be upheld throughout their territories. So it was announced that Sunday was to be a day of rest, kept holy to God, and that no one must work on that day.

The Muslims of Pangaribuan, already resentful, decided that this prohibition could not apply to them. So on Sunday they went out as usual to work in the paddyfields. The raja sent messengers to tell them to stop. As the crowd came by on their way home from church they found the raja's servants shouting at the Muslims to put down their tools. The Muslims only laughed and continued working. With cries of fury the worshippers rushed onto the field, grabbing at the farmers' hoes. The Muslims took fright. Dropping their tools they ran off, soiled and mudstained, all the way to the Dutch district office.

Next day Cleopas was summoned to appear before the Dutch authorities. His accusers charged him with torturing them and pushing them down in the mud.

"I'm sorry about the disturbance," said the pendeta. "But I myself was still in church when the quarrel broke out, because the Sunday service had only just finished."

"Hmm." The Dutch official looked closely at the group of Muslim farmers. "Was it really the minister here who attacked you?"

"We meant the pendeta's men, sir. The people he gave his orders to."

"But I only found out afterwards that you had been working in the paddyfields," Cleopas pointed out. "So how could I give orders for them to ill-treat you?"

He told the official how the church meeting had decided that the Christians and their clans should be forbidden to work on Sunday, in keeping with the Fourth Commandment. The raja of

Pangaribuan had made this a law throughout his kingdom, Cleopas explained, because in Batak tradition all the people in his territory were considered as his kin.

"So according to Batak adat, these people who live in the raja's village should obey his commands."

"Is that true that you live in the raja's village as his people?"

They acknowledged that it was.

"Then why did you not obey his commands?"

Silence.

The official apologized for troubling Cleopas, and then turned sharply to the Muslims. "You've slandered this pendeta. You deserve to be imprisoned yourselves for that!"

But Cleopas interrupted. "Sir, this was only a misunderstanding. Please let them go home to their families. I'm sure it's best if they apologize to the raja and promise that they'll respect his honour in future."

He shook hands with each of the Muslim Bataks in turn, to show his desire to be on good terms with them.

For several months all was quiet. Then one Sunday, as Meisel was riding home from a distant congregation, he saw women planting out rice shoots. He jumped off his horse, holding the reins in one hand, and called to them.

"Ho there! Why are you working on Sunday?"

The women took no notice, but moved calmly along the row, spacing out the young shoots.

Meisel called out again. "Hey! Why don't you answer?"

Still they ignored him.

Thinking that they might not have heard him, the missionary led his horse down on to the little path which ran alongside the paddyfield. He had barely gone a few steps when a group of men leaped out from behind some tall bushes, brandishing guns, knives, spades and sticks. Quickly Meisel jumped on his horse and swung it round. A slashing knife caught the horse's tail and the animal fled like the wind, with a crowd of angry Bataks running behind.

Cleopas was coming home from church when he saw an uproar at the missionary's house. He rushed to call the raja, who came hurrying to see what was happening. They found the door broken open and a crowd of men with staves yelling at the missionary.

The raja's men dashed into the melee. Some of the Muslims ran off, but others stood their ground and one who was clearly the leader pushed his way to the front.

"Our wives were sitting beside the paddyfield," he told the raja, "and this missionary came annoying them. He wants to defile our women now, it seems!"

There was a horrified silence. Meisel stared aghast at the accuser. The raja glared at the Muslims. No one believed the accusation, but no one seemed able to answer it.

"Throw them all out!" said the raja at last.

Muttering angrily, the Muslims made their way home.

"They can't possibly believe that, can they?" whispered Meisel.

Cleopas shook his head. He intensely regretted what had happened. These resentments would not easily be wiped out.

A few nights later there came a banging on Meisel's door.

"Pendeta! Come and help! My wife's sick, and she needs medicine!"

As the missionary opened the door, the man outside took a shot at him. The hammer struck, but for some reason the gun did not fire. The man turned and ran. Trembling all over, Meisel stared out into the night.

"Thank you, Lord," he murmured.

Feelings ran high. The Christians called on the raja to burn down the houses of the Muslims. Steadfastly he refused.

Cleopas told the Christians again and again of the need to live at peace with their neighbours. He visited the leading Muslims whenever he could. They received him graciously, but they would not forget their grievances against the Christians and especially against the white missionary.

Open conflict was avoided, but relationships were never good. Eventually the Muslims decided to move elsewhere.

"Good!" said the raja. "We've got rid of them."

"No," said Cleopas. "We've failed to show them the love of Christ."

THE DEMON SNAKE 14

"Come and join me, Cleopas," called Bishop Nommensen. "I'm watching the boys go by with their little fishing boats."

The two old friends, who were learning to take things a little easier, sat together in silence for a time, enjoying the sunshine by the lakeside. The bishop was in his late seventies by this year of 1911, though still very active. His second wife had died two years before. Nommensen and his youngest daughter lived with his son Jonathan and his family at Sigumpar, where Jonathan was the pendeta. He had asked Cleopas to come and see him.

"You've never been to Samosir Island, have you, Cleopas?" said Nommensen after a while.

"No, Ompu."

It seemed strange, when he had lived for so many years at Lumban Bagasan beside the lake, that he had never visited the island. But Lake Toba could be capricious, more like a small sea than a lake, and Bataks did not lightly cross that dark expanse of water. Nommensen began to talk of his own trips to Samosir, and of the beginnings of Christian congregations there.

The island humped up into an oval-shaped plateau about forty kilometres in length. Its steep sides plunged down sheer to the lake with a narrow fringe at the shoreline here and there, and on the east side the lower slopes opened out more gently to a wide expanse of lowland. Since the nineties a missionary had been based at the south end of Samosir, and he had travelled round the island by boat with the leading raja, putting in at the different villages to preach the gospel. More recently another missionary had been appointed to the northwest where a thin strip of land, like an umbilical cord, joined Samosir to the mainland.

"Quite a large congregation there already," said Nommensen.

He paused to look round at the lake, the glowing paddyfields, and the distant backcloth of green mountains.

"Fifty years since the Mission came to Batakland, Cleopas. And look what the Lord has done!"

Cleopas smiled at the old missionary's beaming face. He was beginning to realize Nommensen's purpose in talking to him about Samosir.

"I would love to see that whole island receiving Christ," said the bishop, "not just a few villages here and there by the water's edge. We've no minister on that whole eastern stretch, although already there's the beginnings of a congregation at Ambarita. They've had visits at different times. And we've a missionary on the mainland opposite now, at Prapat. But we need someone living right there at Ambarita, who can evangelize the villages around and go up to the top of the hillside too."

"Yes, Ompu."

"Would you be willing to go there, Cleopas? It's new territory for you, I know."

Cleopas nodded slowly. "Yes. We'll go there."

"But Cleopas, I think it will be best if you go alone at first."

"Alone?"

"There's no house there for you yet. You'll have to lodge with someone in the village. And I think your wife might find it — well," Nommensen wrinkled his nose, "difficult. You're both getting on now, you know," he added with a wry grin, "and you have a large family. You'd best leave them at Tarutung, in your own village, at least at first."

Cleopas discussed the proposed move with Petronella. They agreed that she should go with the children to their home village of Pulopulo II. It would be a good opportunity to build a family house in preparation for their not-too-distant retirement. Petronella and the boys were given responsibility for organizing the building. Cleopas set off alone for Ambarita.

He spent a couple of weeks first at Prapat with the German missionary, Pendeta Weisenbruch, visiting in the surrounding villages and sharing the gospel. Then Weisenbruch took him across by boat to Ambarita, where the raja, Ompu Pikir, was waiting to welcome them.

After the traditional meal of pork served in its own blood, and the usual welcoming speeches, Cleopas told them it was his desire to share the Christian faith with the people of Ambarita and to bring progress to the island through education. The raja was enthusiastic. He promised that his people would build a teacher's house and a school, and immediately began to calculate, with the help of the village elders, how much each marga and village could be asked to contribute.

Both minister and missionary felt well pleased with this opening. As he stepped on to his boat next morning, Weisenbruch turned back to clasp the pendeta's hand.

"I'll pray for you every day, Cleopas, and do all I can to support your work here. Send me word if there's anything you need."

"Yes, thank you."

He watched the boat shrinking into the distance as it sped across the water to Prapat.

"Come, Pendeta," said the raja. "I want you to meet my nephew."

During the first few weeks the raja took Cleopas visiting almost every day. At each village he introduced the new minister, explained about the proposed school and the benefits this would bring, and collected contributions for the building. Cleopas spoke a little about the Christian faith, how he himself had become a Christian and how God had protected and guided him over the years. Many had heard something of Christianity from occasional visits of missionaries to Ambarita. In a number of places

Cleopas met with such a ready response that he was able to start catechism classes.

In the little town of Ambarita, where there was already an embryo congregation, Cleopas gathered the children for morning school in the sopo. Weisenbruch sent across books and sports equipment, which proved a great spur to the children's enthusiasm. Cleopas told them Bible stories and taught them singing and games as well as the basics of reading, writing and arithmetic.

In less than a month the raja had collected enough money to build both a house and a school. Weisenbruch sent across building materials, and the raja quickly organized the workmen. In two weeks the teacher's house was finished.

"Wonderful!" said Weisenbruch, when Cleopas and Raja Pikir crossed over to Prapat to report on their progress. "If I might suggest it, Ompu Pikir, I think that you should go with Pendeta Cleopas to Sigumpar to tell the bishop himself in person. Then you can ask him to send a teacher straight away for the school."

After spending the night in Prapat, the two Bataks set off round the lake to Sigumpar. Nommensen was delighted to hear that in two short months they had managed to build a teacher's house and find money for a school. Ambarita was said to be too poor to build a church, so that services had to be held in the sopo.

"Truly, Ompu, you must be very rich and powerful," said Nommensen graciously. "Your commands are obeyed as law by your people. So I trust that before long you will be able to build a church and a minister's house too, at Ambarita."

Seeing the raja's startled expression he hurriedly added, "I feel proud and happy, Ompu, at this achievement. I know how many difficulties you have faced, and how much time you have given to this work. May our all-loving Lord bless you and lead you in your service for His glory."

With respectful farewells on both sides, Cleopas and Ompu Pikir departed. Shortly afterwards a teacher was appointed to Ambarita, leaving Cleopas free to concentrate on evangelism and his pastoral ministry.

As he talked with the people of Ambarita, Cleopas gradually discovered that they lived in fear of the huge old banyan tree which dominated the town.

The banyan was considered sacred by the Bataks, and one was usually planted at the founding of a new village. It was a symbol of the Batak "tree of life" and gave shade from the hot sun as well as protection from evil powers. This specimen was ancient, towering high into the sky, its dangling aerial roots trailing like dark tresses around the thickened trunk. The trunk divided into three at shoulder height, so that the spreading canopy covered a wide area. At the point of division a dark hole gaped.

Cleopas went to look at the tree for himself, and gazed in dismay at the offerings left on the ground beneath it — piles of yellow rice garnished with chillies on banana leaves, an arrangement of pink and white petals, a stick of incense burning.

"Please God, none of the Christians have left these," he murmured.

"She mustn't be crossed."

He turned sharply to see an old woman sitting on a bag of paddy, her lips red from chewing the habitual betel nut. She solemnly chewed for a few minutes before gesturing with her chin to the hole in the tree trunk.

"She's a sacred tree with magic powers, and she mustn't be crossed. And in there," with a nod of her chin, "in that hole lives the demon snake!"

"A demon snake?"

The woman nodded vigorously.

"What sort of snake?"

She shrugged. "Very long, very fat, very dangerous. No one must go past that tree. But we leave offerings there so the snake won't harm us."

"But not if we believe in Jesus. Christians don't need to be afraid of evil spirits or demon snakes."

Again the woman shrugged, then spat into the ditch. Her husband came by just then with his spade, fresh from his work in the fields, and together they lifted the bag of paddy up on to her head.

"I was just asking about the banyan tree," said Cleopas, watching them.

"You be careful of that tree, Pendeta," said the old Batak. "It won't be crossed. There's a poisonous snake lives in that tree, with magic powers. No one goes by there."

"But they leave offerings there, I see."

"Well! We don't want the snake to harm us, do we?"

"But we don't need to be afraid of evil powers when we believe in Jesus," said Cleopas earnestly. "That's why I've come here to Ambarita, to tell everyone the good news about Jesus Christ. He's already defeated all the powers of darkness, so if we trust in Him then we don't need to be afraid any more. Come to the service on Sunday and you can learn about the gospel."

But the old woman was already moving off down the road with her heavy load. Her husband gave a curt nod and strode off too. Cleopas watched them with a frown. People had responded with such enthusiasm when he first shared the gospel in Ambarita. But many, it seemed, were like this old couple, bound by their age-old beliefs and fears and quite uninterested in anything new he had to tell.

Cleopas took his problem to the raja.

"It's not right to make offerings to demons or idols, or to worship spirits in trees," he explained. "God hates it when we do that because He alone is worthy of our worship. When people cling to those old beliefs they are blinded to the truth about Christ."

Ompu Pikir agreed that the banyan tree was a stumbling block and that many people had resisted Christianity for fear of antagonizing the spirit who dwelt there.

"The best thing to do would be to summon all your people and order them to chop the old tree down."

Ompu Pikir stared at him. He let out his breath very slowly, lips pursed in a soundless whistle. "It's difficult. Very difficult. You see, we've always been terrified of the spirit that lives there — the spirit of an ancient holy man, long since dead, who has very special powers."

"Ompu!" Cleopas looked at the raja.

"And besides, there really is a snake living in the hollow trunk. I've seen it myself. It's attacked our pigs more than once. And it's a frightening sight, Pendeta. It can crush even a big pig by winding itself tightly round and round and squeezing it till its bones crack. And then it swallows it down whole." He shuddered and gulped. "You don't forget that in a hurry."

"But we must chop the tree down, Ompu."

"That's right, Pendeta. But call out my people to do it? I couldn't."

There was a long pause. Cleopas wondered how many of the new Christians were still afraid of the tree and its occupant. He was a Batak too, in spite of years of training by sceptical western missionaries, and he knew the power of these ancient fears. All the more reason for proving that Christ's power was greater.

"What if I chop down the tree myself?"

"What?" Ompur Pikir stepped back. "What do you mean?"

"Will you give me your permission to chop down the old banyan tree? To get rid of the snake and to show that you are doing away with the old beliefs and receiving Christ?"

Ompu Pikir stood in silence for a long time. Cleopas held his breath.

"Yes. I agree. If we accept Christ we must reject the old ways. It's all right with me. But what about the snake? Don't forget this is a very fierce snake. The devil's own snake!"

"You don't need to worry about that," said Cleopas. "There is a God who is higher and much more powerful, and He will protect me."

The raja could say no more. He agreed to lend Cleopas an axe the next morning.

News that the minister was planning to chop down the old banyan tree spread like a forest fire. As they bathed in the lake that evening the men could talk of nothing else.

"I can't understand how the pendeta could be so bold as to cut down such a sacred tree."

"Me neither."

"There's no doubt about it, he hasn't considered the danger. The spirit will be furious."

"That's what I'm afraid of! And we'll all suffer for it. How dare he come here from outside and put all our lives in danger!"

Most agreed that Cleopas was about to bring a terrible disaster upon them, and they determined to have nothing to do with it. The women grumbled, too, over their cooking pots. But later, in the full contentment of after-supper talk, some expressed a different view.

"Well, I admire him," said the raja's wife. "He's going to show us for himself whether it's really true, this teaching about Jesus Christ that he wants us to believe in."

"But what if it's not true?"

"Well, I hope he'll be safe."

"We'll pray for him, shall we, the way he taught us?"

Alone in his own dark corner of the raja's house, Cleopas also prayed.

Next day the sun shone clear and bright. The air was cool and the lake shimmered blue and white, sparkling in the sun's rays as if a golden carpet had been spread out, embroidered with reflections of the clouds. But in Ambarita the air was tense and solemn.

One by one people drifted out from their houses and stood around in anxious little knots. Cleopas walked slowly but purposefully towards the sacred banyan tree, the borrowed axe in his hand. Silently they watched him swing himself up into the tree, lithely for a man in his fifties. He stood close, for a moment, to the awesome hole, but then began climbing up from branch to branch. He stopped. Loudly singing a hymn of praise to God, he began to swing the axe to and fro, lopping off the smaller branches within reach and dropping them one by one to the ground.

Suddenly a great tremor swept through the crowd, and several women hid their faces. Others stared open-mouthed at the dark hole where the huge trunk branched into three.

The head of the demon snake, disturbed no doubt by all the commotion, emerged slowly from the depths.

The crowd stood transfixed by terror. Such a snake had been known to crush people, too, in its coils. But the python made no move to attack the pendeta, who was hacking away at the tree, singing lustily. It raised its head for a moment, as if watching Cleopas, then shifted its gaze to the ground below, its tongue shooting in and out all the while. Slowly it turned and slithered down the tree trunk, and away into the undergrowth.

As the long body of the snake disappeared from sight the crowd's fear dissipated. There were shouts of laughter, almost hysterical. One man stepped forward with a knife in his hand, ready to climb up and help cut down branches. Several other men rushed home to fetch knives and axes. This was a tree like any other! They sang and laughed with relief as they all helped to bring it down. Soon the remains of the huge old tree lay dismembered on the ground.

"It'll make good firewood," Cleopas assured them.

"Mmm." They stood in groups, unconvinced, wary of violating the once sacred tree. Cleopas took a thick branch and chopped it up into pieces. Ceremonially he handed the bundle of firewood to the raja.

"Ompu Pikir, please take this wood for your fire."

The raja and his wife took a bundle each. Others followed their lead, and soon the whole tree had been parcelled out and disposed of. Cleopas wiped his hands, grinning broadly.

Next Sunday the sopo was filled to overflowing.

"I saw Satan falling like lightening from heaven," read out Cleopas from Luke's Gospel. "I have given you authority to trample on snakes and scorpions, and to overcome all the power of the enemy; nothing will harm you. However..." He pasued to look round at the listening Bataks, many attending the service for the first time. "However, do not rejoice that the spirits submit to you, but rejoice that your names are written in heaven."

Gently he spoke of God's love for each one of them, expressed in the Lord Jesus.

At the end of the service, many people brought out their old charms and magic tokens. Cleopas piled them up in front of the sopo and solemnly set fire to them. All that would not burn, and even the ashes from the fire, he would throw away later in the lake water.

"Do you believe in Jesus now?" he asked.

"Yes, we do."

"So you won't trust any more in the magic power of these objects, or of holy places or magic animals?"

They nodded their agreement.

"The Lord God I've been telling you about," said Cleopas, "He is the same one who created all things: the earth, the sky, the lake and everything in them. There is nothing and no one else who deserves to be worshipped. God alone is the One we believe in, and He can protect us from all danger."

EPILOGUE
SILINDUNG: 1937

"If only ..." Pendeta Cleopas breathed a deep sigh. "If only we could have ended there, on a note of triumph."

His son Lucius looked up from his notepad.

Lucius had been ordained a minister in 1922, and over the years he served in many of the places where Cleopas had first brought the gospel. Everywhere he went he heard stories of his father's exploits in those early days of evangelism. Eventually he wrote them all down. And now, in his father's 82nd year, he tried to visit Cleopas each week, noting down the old man's reminiscences with a view to writing a biography for the family to keep.

"We were so conscious then of God's victory," Cleopas continued. "It was just as if a great weight had been lifted from the people of Ambarita. Suddenly everyone was coming to church and wanting to be baptized. Ompu Pikir used to say they even had more energy to work in the fields because they felt so happy!"

"And so the gospel spread?"

"It spread. We visited all over the island. Schools were built. The rajas always wanted schools. But I remember in one village the raja insisted we should build a church first, and then the school."

"You travelled by boat a lot, didn't you?"

"Oh yes, many places we could only reach by boat. And the lake could be wild at times."

Cleopas sat in silence for a while, remembering. His legs were weak now and his eyesight dim, but his mind was clear and sharp.

"I remember one time we seemed to get caught up in a

whirlwind. We were all terrified! Round and round we whirled, one minute up on the crest of a wave and the next swirling down to the bottom of the current. Almost a crater of water! We clung on to the boat, and I prayed out loud. And then we got them all singing praise songs."

"And you were saved."

"Yes, thank God. The storm died down, and by the time we reached home the water was calm. It made a big impression on Ompu Pikir. More even than chopping down the banyan tree! Suddenly he realized the power of prayer. He was a very prayerful man after that."

"You weren't on Samosir very long, were you, Father?"

Again Cleopas sighed. "Only a year," he said. "Little more than a year." He sat back with his eyes closed. He could see it all so clearly.

Bishop Nommensen had sent for him towards the end of 1912.

"I've just come back from Tarutung," Nommensen had told him, "and I saw your wife and family in Pulopulo II. It seems that Petronella would find it very hard to move to Ambarita. So I think we must place you somewhere else."

Cleopas nodded. He had foreseen this problem.

"You've achieved a lot on Samosir, Cleopas. We have a church established now at Ambarita, and schools opened. But the church at Bonandolok, in the north of your old district of Hullang, is facing real difficulties. You remember we placed a missionary there, Mr Miller?"

Cleopas nodded again.

"He has often asked if you could be sent back there to help him. And your wife would be happy to go to Bonandolok."

"And so you went to Bonandolok?" Lucius broke in on his thoughts.

"Yes. We went. It was hard to leave Samosir when everything was going so well. But I took it as God's will. You were teaching then, Lucius, remember? Only the youngest children were with us. And it was hard. Many had stopped going to church and weren't sending their children to school. Even those still attending church seemed to have lost their enthusiasm." He sighed. "But then, that always was a hard district. You found that out for yourself when you became the pendeta there."

Lucius acknowledged this with a wry grin.

"But we worked at it, Mr Miller and I. And we did see progress. We visited new villages, started new congregations, set up a hospital and helped to get some good roads built. And then everything turned sour!"

Bishop Nommensen had died in May 1918. Cleopas went with Miller to the funeral in Sigumpar. Nommensen had been his spiritual father and Cleopas felt bereft, almost numb with grief. The two men returned to Bonandolok to find an atmosphere of hate and rejection.

While they were away, elections had been held for a new high raja. The man elected by his fellow rajas was appointed by the Dutch authorities as the new administrative head of the district, following the Dutch policy of governing through the local leadership. The man chosen was not a Christian.

"That was a bitter time," recalled Cleopas. "The rajas who lost the election blamed Miller. Accused him of influencing the appointment, of all things! They stopped coming to church, because they said it had done them no good. The schools emptied and we had to close them down. The nurse was no longer needed at the hospital because everyone was going to the datu instead. Even for weddings, they no longer wanted the church's blessing. They married their sons and daughters when and how the datu told them to, and that was that!"

"But not everyone left."

"No. Some were faithful. The raja of Bonandolok for one, even though he was one of the disappointed rajas. Maybe about forty families were faithful. We met in church each week and we prayed and prayed that God would lift that black cloud that seemed to hover over the whole district."

"And gradually He did. Numbers picked up again."

"Mmm. A little."

They fell silent.

Lucius remembered the dark depression his father had suffered at that time; bereavement partly, the grief of losing someone who had been father, mentor, friend, for so many years. The resentments and misunderstandings in Bonandolok, coming just then, had been too much to bear.

Weighed down by a deep sense of failure, Cleopas had often been sick during those years. Eventually, in 1925, the bishop had agreed that Cleopas should retire. He was almost seventy years old.

"I've thought so often since then," he told Lucius, "how much better it would have been if I could have ended my ministry somewhere else. At Ambarita say, or Pangaribuan. Somewhere where I could see the fruits of my work, where I'd struggled through and overcome the obstacles. Instead of at Bonandolok and failure."

"But don't say failure, Father! God blessed your ministry! Remember the old prophecy, when you were born? The spirits trembled, because they knew you would destroy their rule and the power of the old beliefs, and lead the Bataks into a new teaching. And they were right to be afraid. Because that's just what you did. You and all those other early evangelists, and Ompu Nommensen and the other missionaries. All over the Batak highlands God's kingdom has been proclaimed. The beginning of the end of Satan's rule!"

Cleopas smiled. "Ompu Nommensen had a vision," he remembered. "A vision of churches all around Lake Toba and Christians singing God's praises."

"And it came true."

"Yes, it came true." He sighed and patted his son's hand. "The beginning of God's kingdom in Batakland."

After Lucius had left, Cleopas sat brooding in the gathering twilight. If only ...

Why couldn't I have retired then, after Ambarita, when we had seen the powers of darkness overthrown? When I was seeing fruitfulness in my ministry. But no! It was just in the very place where I felt most downcast. When I struggled and the fruit had not yet come. At a time of failure. Just then the Lord brought my service to a close. Why? ... Why?

At that moment, out of the deep darkness, he heard a voice. "So that you would not glorify yourself!"

POSTSCRIPT

Cleopas' heart might have risen if he could have seen what his Batak Church would become. With a membership of one and a half million, the Batak Protestant Christian Church (Huria Kristen Batak Protestant or HKBP) is now by far the biggest Church in Indonesia, and probably in the whole of South East Asia. Hundreds of thousands more belong to churches which arose out of HKBP.

Batak Christians have not remained isolated in their beautiful mountainous area of North Sumatra. The Church's missionary arm, which began by evangelizing still-animistic areas of the Batak heartlands, also sent missionaries to other parts of Sumatra, to the outlying islands and even to Malaya. In 1957 there was one Batak church in Jakarta — today there are about a hundred. Batak churches witness for Christ in all the main cities of Indonesia, and even in the USA.

The earliest schools and hospitals were built and run by missionaries. Because of this, and because of the go-getter character of the Bataks, Batak Christians have become well educated and risen to hold influential positions in government and society. This is still true today.

In an old church born out of a mass movement, many are inevitably nominal Christians without a heart experience of Christ. Among the younger generation in the cities, new life is growing as the Holy Spirit continues His work. When a Batak catches fire, he is really devoted to the Lord! The Overseas Missionary Fellowship is working alongside Batak Christians and other mission groups to encourage this new life.

If you have enjoyed and been moved by this story of a Batak pioneer missionary, please respond in prayer for the Batak Church today. To obtain more information, write to the addresses at the beginning of this book.

GLOSSARY

Adat	Batak customary law and tradition
Bagasan	The chief of a group of small fortified villages; sometimes used of the group as a whole.
Boru	Daughter. The term is extended to her husband and his family.
Datu	A mixture of priest, magician, doctor, fortune teller
Horas	Traditional Batak greeting with wide meaning (long life, good luck, etc)
Hula-hula	Father-in-law; the family who give their daughter in marriage
Huta	Town, group of villages
Imam	Muslim priest or prayer leader in the mosque
Lumban	Village, usually walled, with bamboo hedge
Marga	Clan
Nyonya	Mrs. A title of respect given to wealthy women
Ompu	Grandfather. Used as a title of respect
Pangulabalang	Spirit of dead child, thought to dwell in a magic substance made from the child's body, and to fight the enemies of its "masters".
Pendeta	Minister
Piso	Gift traditionally given by the bridegroom's family to the bride's parents
Pupuk	Magic substance made from a child's body
Raja	King, chieftain, head of village
Sarung	Length of cloth stitched together at the ends, worn tucked round the waist or under armpits
Sopo	Building where young unmarried men sleep, also used as meeting place. Rice was stored in the roof, and the bones of ancestors.
Tondi	Spirit or soul
Ulos	Special Batak shawl or blanket

BIBLIOGRAPHY

Cleopas Lumbantobing's son Lucius prepared notes for a biography, but it was his grandson, K M L Tobing, who completed the book published in Indonesian (by YKBK/OMF) with the title *Misionaris Lokal*. This English version is based on the author's original manuscript. I have also made use of the books listed below, especially the biography of Nommensen.

My own understanding of Batak history has been helped by many conversations during the course of our ministry in Sumatra. I am grateful for all who have helped me, but realize that I am still a foreigner, and apologize for the consequent shortcomings of this book.

J R Hutauruk: "Pendeta Kleopas Lumbantobing lulusan Sekokah Pendeta gelombang kedua 1887-1889", in *Ketika Aku di dalam Penjara* Pematang Siantar: Grafina 1982.

E M Loeb: *Sumatra: its History and People*: Kuala Lumpur; Oxford University Press 1972

M A Marbun dan I M T Hutapea: *Kamus Budaya Batak Toba*: Jakarta: Balai Pustaka 1987

J T Nommensen: *Ompu i Dr Ingwer Ludwig Nommensen*: Jakarta: BPK Gunung Mulia 1974

P B Pedersen: *Batak Blood and Protestant Soul*: Grand Rapids: Eerdmans 1970

A A Sitompul: *Perintis Kekristenan di Sumatra Bagian Utara*: Jakarta: BPK Gunung Mulia 1986

Ph O L Tobing: *The Structure of the Toba-Batak Belief in the High God*: Amsterdam: Jacob van Campen 1963

Other Biographies Published by OMF

MOUNTAIN RAIN by *Eileen Crossman*
A fresh look at the life of J O Fraser by his daughter Eileen Crossman. She portrays her father's deep devotion to God as he reaches the Lisu people in the southwest mountains of China. The power of prayer from the homelands in breaking Satan's hold over these hill people has been studied by students of missions throughout the world.

TO A DIFFERENT DRUM by *Pauline Hamilton*
The autobiography of Pauline Hamilton. "Grabbing my sickle from the table, Mike began to run. I tore right after him — I wasn't going to have him kill his father with my sickle!" Why had Pauline Hamilton, a physiology PhD, chosen to march to a different drum from her contemporaries, to experience danger and hardship in China and Taiwan? Only because the God who saved her from suicide and gave meaning to her life had called, and as she obeyed she found Him faithful beyond all expectation.

BY SEARCHING by *Isobel Kuhn*
An autobiography with a difference, remarkable for its honesty and frankness. BY SEARCHING portrays Isobel's determined journey from agnosticism to faith. "The freshest, most human and most spiritual piece of autobiography that has been published for many a long day."

NEVER SAY CAN'T by *Linnet Hinton*
Obedience to God's call led Norman and Amy McIntosh to the high grasslands of Tibet, through the green jungles of Malaya and into the congested cities of tropical Asia. They lived through wars, rejection, separation and bereavement, and experienced the joy of fruitful service. Consistently pushed into jobs too big for them, they learned the secret of utter dependence on God.

Other Books About Asian Christians

AS THE ROCK FLOWER BLOOMS by *Rosemary Watson*
Peng was the son of a spirit priest in Laos. His Taway tribe had a tradition that when the lichen on the rocks began to bloom, the unknown Good Spirit was about to send deliverance from the powers of evil. Peng desperately wanted to be delivered, and this book tells the true story of his search, his discovery, and the subsequent transformation of his life and that of his family.

THE WIND IS HOWLING by *Ayako Miura*
This autobiography penetrates deeply into Japanese attitudes and life. Mrs Miura explains her own pathway to Christ through the turbulent post-war years.

MORE THAN SKIN DEEP by *Margaret Armitage*
This true story of the treatment of Lamon, a leprosy patient in rural Thailand beautifully transformed from the inside, will inspire those facing their own difficult circumstances.

WITHOUT A GATE by *Jean Nightingale*
Through the eyes and feelings of A Tsa and his wife A Peh you will experience the trauma and freedom that comes when Christ and His Church enter an Akha village in North Thailand.